MURDER
TO SCALE

MURDER TO SCALE

a novel

DEBRA B. SCHIFF

With Mike Blumensaadt, MMR

PHILADELPHIA
2018

Library of Congress Control Number: 2017915991
ISBN 978-0-6929662-4-2

ACKNOWLEDGMENTS

I want to thank the following people: Debra Balke, MD, Board of Directors, The Central Coast Autism Spectrum Center, for validating my depiction of autism; Doug Blaine, for his invaluable comments and unwavering support; Mike Blumensaadt, for taking a chance on helping a total stranger with this book, his inventive layouts, and his technical advice throughout the process; Doug Gordon, for his insightful editing, skilled typography, and vital guidance through the publishing process; Joan Heigh, a kind editor and treasured friend, without whose encouragement this book *never* would have been written or come together; Tony Koestler, for early suggestions; David L. Pine, LLC, for criminal procedure advice; my beloved husband, Stanley Platt, for his steadfast confidence in me; Cindy Rudy, proofreader extraordinaire; Geoff Shannon, for his creative cover design; and all the many model railroaders I have met over the years who welcomed me into the hobby with open arms and who continue to amaze me with their talent and creativity. One thing is no mystery: why model railroading is the World's Greatest Hobby[SM]!

CHAPTER 1

It was a warm day for early December in central Pennsylvania. Hard to believe there's only 21 more days until Christmas, Tom McCloud thought as he carefully loaded his modular model train layout into the back of his royal blue Ford pickup. The layout had been specifically designed to be moved so it could be attached to other layouts to create one big holiday train wonderland. Although it was packaged in a special crate, he still made sure it was secured with plenty of heavy blankets so it wouldn't bounce around in transit. As he went back in the house to pick up his work bag, he barely glanced at his reflection—hazel eyes, neatly combed short gray hair, and matching mustache—in the hallway mirror. He plucked his tan Central PA Model Railroad Club baseball cap off a peg, while Lady, his cocker spaniel-beagle, barked excitedly.

"Sorry, girl, you can't come along on this trip," Tom said, petting her silky head. He made a quick escape out the front door.

The sunny 55° weather had not dampened his holiday spirit. He found himself whistling "Jingle Bells" while backing down his driveway. Why shouldn't I be in the holiday mood?

he thought—after all, I'm driving to set up our annual Christmas display. He never got tired of watching children's expressions as they walked around the intricate display in the basement of St. Mark's Lutheran Church with its 100 feet of track, multiple trains, over 200 figures, and elaborate holiday scenery. Tom felt a familiar twinge in his gut when he thought about how much his wife Claire used to enjoy watching the awe-struck children. He had promised himself not to dwell on those memories and managed to push the thought out of his mind.

It was only a 15-minute drive to the church. He passed through Pennsville's five-block downtown area, decorated with garland-wrapped light poles and overhead banners announcing special holiday hours. At 8:00 am, none of the stores were open yet. The usual congregation of pickups lined the front of the Busy Bee Cafe where the regulars were gossiping over their morning coffee and pork roll omelets.

Pulling into the church parking lot, he saw Bill Murphy's meticulously restored 1960 aquamarine T-Bird. Bill was one of the three other modelers who were bringing layout sections and trains. Tom decided to go say hello to him before wrestling his own section down to the church basement. Tom had brought a Thermos of coffee along. He looked forward to sharing a cup with Bill and chewing over the logistics of the setup before they settled into work.

The back door leading directly down to the basement was unlocked. The church janitor usually got to the building early, turned on the lights, and left the door open for the layout crew while he worked in the chapel upstairs. Since it was a Saturday, the train modelers would have the run of the large all-purpose room to themselves.

Tom bounded down the steps, eager to see Bill's contributions for this year's program. He was barely across the room's threshold before he froze in his tracks. Bill was seated in a chair with his back to Tom, his head down on a work table at an awkward angle with his arms dangling. Tom's first thought was that Bill had suffered a heart attack. No matter how often Bill swore to turn over a new leaf, it had been obvious to his friends that he was fighting a losing battle against jelly doughnuts and a two-pack-a-day smoking habit.

When Tom got closer, he saw that the crown of Bill's balding scalp was almost caved in, leaving a gaping wound. A torrent of blood had flowed down Bill's faded denim shirt, forming a pool under his head. He raced over to check Bill's pulse. Although his arm still felt warm, there was no pulse and Bill was not breathing. There was no question that his friend was dead. His heart pounding, Tom called 911.

"This is 911. Where are you and what is the nature of your call?" the female dispatcher calmly asked.

"I'm in the basement of St. Mark's Lutheran Church, corner of Main and Norris Avenues, Pennsville. Please send help. There's been a murder." Even as Tom said the word aloud, it seemed totally unreal. Murder was something that happened in big cities or on *Law and Order,* not in Pennsville and certainly not to someone like Bill Murphy.

"Okay. I need your name and a callback number. Please do not hang up the phone."

After Tom identified himself and gave her his cell phone number, the dispatcher continued asking questions. "You said there's been a murder. Are you sure the person is not breathing?"

Tom described Bill's condition, assuring the dispatcher that there was no question that the victim had drawn his last breath.

"Get yourself to a safe place, sir. The police will be right there."

Tom cautiously looked around. There was nowhere a killer could hide in the brightly lit room. Tom knew enough not to touch anything else as his brain slowly processed that he was looking at a crime scene. People don't accidentally hit the back of their heads and fall forward onto a table. He saw Bill's steel toolbox on the floor, a huge dent in its corner that appeared to be covered with blood, hair, and bits of something else Tom didn't want to think about. Before he could explore the rest of the room, he was met by Pennsville's Chief of Police, Ben Taylor. Chief Taylor presided over a 13-person force with a lieutenant, 2 sergeants, a detective, and 9 police officers. The Pennsville police usually dealt with a light load of small-town crimes—petty larceny, teenage vandalism, the occasional brawl at Frank's Roadhouse, and a few cases of domestic violence. They had been friends since grammar school, so Tom couldn't help but think of him as "Ben" first and "Chief Taylor" second. Their wives were also friends, and the couples had often gotten together for dinner or a backyard barbecue. Ben still had the muscular 6'4", 225-

pound frame that had tackled Tom too many times to count during high school varsity football games.

The normally easygoing Chief looked uncharacteristically grim as he approached Tom and took in the scene.

"I'm sorry, Tom. I know Bill was your friend." He took Tom gently by the arm and steered him toward a police officer standing by the doorway. "You're going to have to wait outside. Officer Logan will take your statement."

When they emerged into the sunlight, Tom swayed slightly as what he had just witnessed fully hit him. Officer Logan led Tom to a bench on the church's lawn and suggested he sit there. Tom took some deep breaths of fresh air. When Tom's color had returned and he stood without wobbling, the officer briskly questioned him. Why was he here? What time had he arrived? Did he see anyone else anywhere near the church? Tom haltingly answered in as much detail as he could muster.

While Tom was being questioned, the whole block had been surrounded by yellow caution tape printed repeatedly with "Police — Crime Scene" in bold black letters. The parking lot was filled with flashing lights from a variety of police cars from other law enforcement agencies, an ambulance, and the cars of forensic investigators who had arrived to process the scene. Although he had been enjoying the warm temperature when he started out that morning, Tom now was shivering. After what seemed like an eternity, the officer finished asking his questions. He reviewed his notes before looking back up at Tom.

"Mr. McCloud, could you please stay put until we give you permission to leave."

Although it was said politely, Tom knew it was an order, meant to be obeyed. He couldn't tell if he was actually considered a suspect. It seemed too ludicrous to be true. But then again, he now understood how Alice must have felt when she tumbled down the rabbit hole.

As he waited, the medical examiner exited the building, rolling out a black body bag that was placed in the back of the state examiner's vehicle. Tom realized that part of him had been holding out hope for a medical miracle. That somehow the wound was superficial and Bill could be brought back to consciousness by an EMT's expert CPR. The zipped-up body bag made Bill's death only too real. Tom thought about Bill's wife Annie and their three daughters. He would miss Bill's mischievous sense of humor that helped enliven the Central PA Model Railroad Club meetings. He couldn't imagine how Annie and their kids would handle it.

After what seemed a lifetime to Tom, but was really another 45 minutes, the forensic examiner left the basement carrying several large paper bags that must have contained potential physical evidence. With the examiner finished processing the scene, Tom thought he would at last be free to go.

Chief Taylor stood in the parking lot conferring with a State Police captain. The Chief then gave orders to the rest of his men, several of whom spread out to sweep the area for any possible witnesses. Once the officers were dispersed, Chief Taylor finally came over to talk to him. "Tom, I am going to take you back inside so you can survey the basement and check if anything of Bill's was taken. Remember, don't touch anything."

"Sure, Ben. I'll do whatever it takes to help catch the bastard who did this."

As the Chief closely watched him, Tom looked over the quarter section of train layout that had been placed on the table. It was in HO scale (1:87 ratio, or 87 times smaller than actual trains). Bill's section featured a winter sports scene complete with ski slope, ski lift, ice skating rink, chalets, and an Alpine-style hotel. Once set up, the scene would be filled with realistic skiers coming down the slopes and riding the ski lift, with colorful ice skaters taking some turns on the "frozen" pond. And because Bill could not resist adding a comic touch, there was an unlikely polar bear in the corner threatening some oblivious outdoor hot tubbers. Bill had spent hours putting together the Faller Alpine chalet and hotel kits. He had even inserted a mountain cableway for added realism.

A second module, being brought later by Gordon Brendam, featured Pennsville as it would have looked in the 1950s, with an old-fashioned train station and a main street of Design Preservation Model buildings. He had also labored putting together a Christmas village of quaint stores with twinkling lighted display windows. The town and station would be blazoned with Christmas lights and a large decorated tree that drew a crowd to the park. The streets would be filled with holiday shoppers. Tom knew that Gordon preferred to model Civil War–era N scale steam (1:160 to prototype), but as a hobby shop owner, he was an expert in all scales. One of the layout shops subtly advertised his own "Pennsville Toy and Hobby Store."

A third section would feature a large 1950s city, prototypical Union station, and train shed in front of a module Christmas parade that marched between the station and detailed city backdrop. This was James Spencer's project. He loved electric trains and ran a classic streamlined Pennsylvania GG-1 locomotive on his layout. James had started out modeling old O scale Lionel and Williams trains (1:48), but had switched to Digital Command Control (DCC) HO. He liked to keep up with the newest and the best in model trains as well as everything else he managed.

Tom modeled more for fun than realism. His module featured a Santaland, sidings for a reindeer barn, a toy factory, and Santa's house. The child-pleasing Thomas the Tank Engine™, a bright blue steam engine from the popular books and films, would be busy moving fun cars, such as an animated stock car with reindeer heads that bobbed out the windows as the car went around the track.

The diverse Christmas layout that would combine both realistic and whimsical sections summarized everything Tom loved about the hobby. It had something for everyone and let every individual find his own creative niche. He couldn't believe Bill wouldn't be around to enjoy this year's holiday magic.

Bill's module sat on a long wooden table. Bill had already placed his 2-8-0 locomotive on the far side of the track. (Steam locomotives are classified by the Whyte notation system. The first number is the leading wheels; the second, the driving wheels; and the third, the number of wheels on the trailing end of the locomotive.) He must still have been in the process of unwrapping the rolling stock from their protective packaging when the killer struck. For the Christmas module, Bill ran this green Southern Baldwin 2-8-0 locomotive (known as a "Consolidation") that he kept in gleaming, unweathered shape to use for the holidays. Many modelers painstakingly "weathered" their trains with different finishes such as rust, water streaks, or dirt lines so they would look more like the actual prototypes. This shiny steam locomotive would pull 20 different cars, including hoppers hand-painted with festive holiday decorations such as candy canes and gingerbread men; tank cars transporting hot cocoa and eggnog; and gondolas filled with tiny wrapped presents. A snowman with a top hat and red scarf that had not yet been placed on the layout sat forlornly on the table. Bill's track voltage tester, lubrication bottles, and track cleaner that were usually scattered about had disappeared, probably into one of the forensic examiner's paper bags. More strikingly, Bill's dented steel workbox was gone. Tom surmised this was probably one of the most important pieces of evidence for the forensic examiner.

As he surveyed the room, Tom noticed an unusually long display case sitting on a high shelf. The empty case had an engraved nameplate that he couldn't make out. It must have contained Bill's prized scratch-built 2-8-8-8-2 steam locomotive (known as the Erie Triple 8 or Triplex). The 2-8-8-8-2 was out of place at this Christmas-themed display. However, the model had won First Place "People's Choice Locomotive" and First Place "Scratch Built Locomotive" awards at the summer National Model Railroad Association (NMRA) convention and Bill had told James, Gordon, and Tom that he was bringing it. Tom suspected that he wanted to get a rise out of James and Gordon, although Gordon was a Master Model Railroader (MMR) who had scratch-built his own award-winning models. An MMR is a member of the NMRA who has obtained at least 7 of the 11 Achievement Certificates in the association's Achievement Program. It is so difficult to obtain that fewer than 600 members have received it since the program started in 1961.

Now the Triplex was nowhere to be seen. It looked like the murderer had panicked and grabbed the Triplex but left the 2-8-0 and a *Polar Express* set that was to be raffled off still sitting on the table closest to the door. While the Triplex was by far the more valuable locomotive, something didn't seem right about this, but Tom couldn't quite put his finger on it.

Ben interrupted Tom's thoughts to ask him if he noticed anything missing. It forced Tom to focus on the concrete ways he could help his deceased friend.

"It looks like only one steam locomotive, what is known as a Triplex, is gone. It is probably worth about $1500, if the thief could find a way to sell it," Tom replied. "It seems like such a pittance for a man's life."

"*Nothing* is worth a man's life," Ben said angrily. "We'll turn over every rock to find the sleaze ball who did this. It's unfortunate the church does not have any security cameras."

Once they got outside, Ben called Officer Logan over. "Mr. McCloud is going to give you a detailed description of a missing locomotive. We need to check every pawn shop within 60 miles as well as online auction sites."

"Tom, what's going on? Why can't I come in?"

Tom looked across the lot to see James Spencer standing outside the police barricade being blocked by a determined police officer. A short man with thick curly black hair and a whiny voice, he always reminded Tom of a high-strung poodle. James was the owner of several of the area's biggest businesses, including a jewelry store, real estate agency, and car dealership, and thought he deserved a certain deference from Pennsville's citizens. He was also president of the model railroading club.

"I'm sure it is something important or they would let us go in," someone hidden behind the officer was soothingly telling James. Tom recognized the voice of Gordon, the creator of the fourth piece of the Christmas layout. Gordon had an autistic teenage son, Donnie. Over the years, the slow, gentle tone he needed to keep his son calm had become his normal way of addressing everyone. A mild-looking man who resembled the actor William H. Macy, he was as laidback as James was wired.

After Chief Taylor gave his permission, Tom went over to talk to James and Gordon. James didn't wait for Tom to reach him before demanding, "OK, what's going on here? I'm ready to set up my layout."

Chief Taylor looked at Tom and nodded. Tom swallowed hard and then looked both of his friends in the eye. "It's Bill. He's been murdered."

"That's ridiculous," said James. "Who would possibly want to harm Bill? It *must* have been some kind of accident."

"Let's just say this is an active crime scene. All we know at this point is that Mr. Murphy is deceased," Chief Taylor replied. He sounded poised and professional, but Tom knew by Ben's rigid posture that the Chief was keeping his temper in check.

"Oh, it probably was a robbery by a desperate drug addict that went terribly wrong. It makes sense that the police can't go into details now," Gordon interjected, as usual breaking some of the tension his friend James was oblivious to causing. "How very sad, though. I'm sure the police will find out who did this." He turned to Tom, "I guess we are holding on to our layouts. This will be hard to explain to the children who were looking forward to seeing our display. If you don't mind, I want to get going. I have Donnie waiting alone in the car."

Ignoring the Chief, James told Tom, "I'm going to set up a special club meeting for Tuesday night. We need to send our official condolences to Bill's family. Then we need to see when we can put up our Christmas display. Yes, there are many details I must attend to." Feeling in charge again and ready to throw around his weight as club president, James rushed away from the scene.

After the two had gone, the Chief told Tom he could also leave. "But remember, it's important to contact us immediately if you think of any other details you didn't tell me or Officer Logan."

Chief Taylor went over to talk to the officers who had returned from sweeping the neighborhood for witnesses. Officer Logan had already interrogated the janitor. The Chief would have to talk to church officials about suspending their normal Sunday services because the church was now a crime scene that couldn't be disturbed, even for a good cause.

Tom trudged back to his truck. Although he had only been there a little over an hour, it seemed like it was days ago that he arrived at the church, eager to spread the holiday spirit through model railroading. Now that he was alone, he realized what was bothering him about the missing Triplex. Why would a thief who knew nothing about model railroading reach up to a high shelf to grab a weathered train that looked like it had been around forever and would be awkward to carry with its multiple wheels and tender when he could have grabbed the shiny, smaller 2-8-0 that was right in front of him? Better yet, why not just steal a boxed Christmas train set that he could have sold on the street for fast cash? Of course that was assuming the thief was not a model railroader. But if the thief was a model railroader, maybe this wasn't an act of random violence after all.

CHAPTER 2

Tom went through the rest of the day doing his usual errands on autopilot. When he was putting away a can of tomato puree from a grocery shopping trip, he caught his breath. The red label reminded him too much of a puddle of blood. The disturbing possibilities about Bill's murder played out in Tom's mind as he drove out to the Good Shepherd Nursing Home to see Claire. In a strange way, he was grateful to have the crime to focus on rather than the sadness he felt on his daily visits to see his Alzheimer-stricken wife. As painful as it was to see his wife of 38 years who no longer recognized him, it would be more painful not to give her a kiss as he had done every night of their marriage. They had never even slept a night apart until the disease had made it impossible for him to continue to care for her at home. That fact had been driven home when she had wandered out of bed one night and then fallen and broken her hip. Once she was in rehabilitation, the medical staff had convinced him that it would be better for Claire to live somewhere with 24-hour care. He still felt that he had let her down somehow, even though Good Shepherd was providing her with excellent care.

"Hello, Mr. McCloud, how are you this evening?" the always cheerful receptionist greeted him. "I am so sorry to hear about your friend Bill Murphy."

There had been a brief press conference held by the Chief of Police, a State Police spokesperson, and the Mayor to discuss the murder. No new details were forthcoming. Thankfully Tom was not mentioned as the person who had found the body. However, the murder had become the hot topic of conversation at the Busy Bee Cafe, the Main Street Hair Salon, Pennsville Barber Shop, and Frank's Roadhouse. It never failed to amaze him how quickly news spread in Pennsville. And everyone knew that Tom and Bill had been friends.

"Thanks," Tom responded. He could tell the receptionist wanted to press him for more details, but he didn't break stride as he went over to the elevator. When he got off at Claire's floor, the nurse at the nursing station greeted Tom warmly, but mercifully she was a no-nonsense person focused on the tasks at hand rather than Pennsville gossip.

"So, how's our girl this evening?" Tom asked. Claire had good days and bad days, although lately it seemed that the bad days were becoming more of the norm.

"She ate all three meals today, especially enjoying the chocolate ice cream at dinner."

Tom had to smile. That sounded like the chocoholic Claire that Tom knew and loved. He had always wondered why all those calories never caught up with her petite frame. It must have been because she had been a ball of energy, whether teaching first grade or cooking and cleaning around the house. When he entered her room, her back was to him as she sat in her wheelchair. He still felt a catch in his throat when he saw the graceful curve of her neck. He had to remember he could not sneak up and move her braid of soft gray hair to kiss her on the neck as he had done countless times during their marriage. When he walked around to face her, she looked as beautiful to him as ever; however, her lovely blue eyes that used to be brimming with good nature were blank. She wrinkled her brow in concentration and then smiled as she said, "Hello, Doug. I knew you would come to see me. Your father never does. When are you taking me home?"

Tom had learned not to contradict her. It was better that she enjoyed a visit with their son Doug, who had moved to Arizona three years ago.

After kissing her on the cheek, he pulled over a chair so he could sit down and hold her hand. "Oh, you know, I'm sure Dad will be here soon."

"That job is killing him. I wish he would quit soon."

It had been two years since Tom had taken early retirement from his job as a highway engineer at PennDOT, the state's Department of Transportation, to care for her.

"I need to go home right now. You know he can't manage without me. Go speak to the nurse right now," Claire demanded.

Tom knew the visit was over. If he didn't go

and pretend to speak to a nurse, Claire would become more and more agitated. When he peeked back in 20 minutes later, she was sound asleep. He sat down and told her everything that happened that day, including his doubts that Bill's murder was a drug robbery gone wrong. How he wished he had his old Claire back as a sounding board. While Tom knew how parts fit together, Claire understood what made people tick.

CHAPTER 3

The Central PA Model Railroad Club was meeting under tense circumstances three days after the murder. Members had to walk through a gauntlet of TV reporters trying to interview them about Bill Murphy's death. Only a few people stopped to spout the usual clichés about what a nice quiet town Pennsville was and how nothing like this ever happened here. James made sure he was interviewed and gave a Chamber of Commerce–worthy speech extolling the virtues of Pennsville. Once inside, members stood around in small knots of two or three in the fluorescent-lit back room of American Legion Post #244, discussing Bill Murphy's death in hushed tones over the faint buzz of the heating system. Many of the members tried to buttonhole Tom since he had been at the crime scene. At least the police hadn't let anyone know that he had been the one to discover the body. They also hadn't released details about the Triplex being taken. Tom sidestepped the probing questions and just kept telling everyone that he didn't really know any more than they did.

James marched in and headed straight for the podium at the front of the room. He clapped his hands and asked everybody to take their seats so the meeting could get started. The 15 or so modelers parked themselves in the rows of tan folding chairs. After the club secretary hurried through old business, the club was ready to discuss the business of the evening.

"As you all know, our beloved member Bill Murphy has passed away under horrific circumstances."

"He didn't seem that beloved to you when he disagreed with you, you big fake," someone muttered in the row behind Tom.

James continued, not indicating that he had heard the comment, "I know many of you will be at his wake tomorrow night and then his funeral on Friday. I thought it would be an appropriate gesture if we provide a floral arrangement for the funeral. Norman Knapp, owner of Norman's Natural Florists, has offered to provide the wreath at a generous discount. All in favor say 'aye.' All opposed say 'nay.' The ayes have it," James noted.

"Next up is the issue of the Christmas display at St. Mark's. We have been notified that the downstairs will be open starting next Wednesday night. Unfortunately, that means our display will only be up for two weeks before Christmas and the week after Christmas until New Year's Day."

Tom listened with one ear as he thought about Bill's death. If it was true that the murderer had specifically grabbed the Triplex, then it was possible that he was sitting somewhere in this room. Tom slowly scanned the attentive faces, not sure what he was looking for. He knew that the murderer hadn't sprouted horns. Once again, he was struck by all the gray and graying heads surrounding him. One reason everyone tolerated James' pompous air was the hope that because he was 40, he might be able to bring in some younger members.

Tom had been hooked on model railroading from the time he received his first Lionel train on his eighth birthday. When he got older, he liked the hands-on aspects of the hobby that let him use his electrical wiring and carpentry skills. Even when he felt overwhelmed while starting his career and spending every spare moment with his infant son, he had always taken pleasure in at least running a train around the Christmas tree. Tom's son, Doug, had been a huge *Thomas & Friends*™ fan as a child. Some hobbyists joked that Thomas was a gateway "drug" to a modeling addiction. However, as Doug got older, he had not bonded with Tom over "real" trains as Tom had hoped. Doug had been more interested in video games. Tom was hoping that now that he was a grandfather, he would get another chance at having a modeler in the family. He knew Bachmann Trains, a major model train manufacturer, had introduced a new app that let users control trains through their smart phones. Maybe this was the way to get today's tech-centered generation interested in the hobby. After all, their whole lives seemed to revolve around their phones. And can't we blame ourselves, Tom wondered, when some of the "rivet counters" (modelers who demanded exact adherence to every aspect of prototypical trains) would not let children touch their trains. Tom firmly believed that modelers should do whatever they wanted to do with their own railroads that made them happy—even if it meant making up a roadname (the train company's name shown on an engine) or running locomotives with the "wrong" cars (known as freelancing).

Which brought him back to the missing Triplex. Could a hobbyist obsessed by collecting have read about Bill's prize-winning project and been consumed with owning it? Maybe they had argued after Bill refused to sell it and hitting him over the head was a crime of passion.

Whoa, don't let your imagination get carried away, Tom chided himself, realizing that the club meeting had ended. You're an engineer, and engineers solve problems by looking at facts. He was saved from any more wild ideas by James bringing over a new member to talk to him. Tom had a reputation of being remarkably patient when dealing with newcomers to the hobby.

"Ryan Stafford, this is Tom McCloud. He'll be happy to answer any of your questions." James left before Ryan could get a word out. Although James talked a good game about increasing membership, he never seemed to have the time for working with potential members.

If Ryan, an earnest-looking man in his late 40s wearing a Pittsburgh Steelers cap and sweatshirt, was put off by the president's abrupt departure, he didn't let on. "Hi, Tom. I'm looking to get back into the hobby after dabbling in it in my youth, but so much has seemed to change. I'm not sure whether to run DC or DCC-equipped trains." (DCC users run their engines by using a digital controller that "speaks" to a decoder in each engine; DC, or direct current, works by providing power directly to the track.) Tom quizzed Ryan about how he envisioned running his trains, what scale he was interested in, and what kind of budget he wanted to start out with. Tom methodically went over the advantages and disadvantages of each type of system until he saw Ryan stifling a yawn.

"I guess that should give you a pretty good idea of what's involved. Sorry I talked so long, but I really do love the hobby."

"Nah, it's just been a long day. I appreciate the advice. It has given me a lot to mull over."

Tom walked Ryan out the door. As they shook hands in the parking lot, Tom couldn't resist telling him: "Remember, model railroading is a lot like the Marines. We're always looking for a few good men . . . and women."

"I'll keep that in mind," Ryan laughed as he got into his car.

Tom hoped he would see Ryan again. Not only because Ryan seemed like a nice guy, but because Tom was determined to keep the hobby that he loved alive, even if he had to do it one person at a time. It seemed he was always defending modelers against the stereotype of a loner who would rather sit in the basement playing with trains than ever step foot in a sports bar and hang out with his buddies. And if a hobbyist had really killed Bill for his engine, that made his argument that modelers were not wild-eyed fanatics much less convincing.

CHAPTER 4

Chief Taylor was already at his favorite booth at the Busy Bee when Tom arrived at 7:30 the next morning. Tom said hello to some of the regulars strung along the counter like a flock of roosting starlings before sliding in across from his friend. The waitress came over with a pot of coffee and filled the thick white mug in front of Tom and refilled the Chief's mug in one experienced motion.

"Good morning, Tom. What'll it be?"

"Nothing else for me. Thanks, Molly."

"I'm good," Ben said, mopping up the last of his over-easy eggs with some toast.

"I thought Rose wanted you to cut back on your cholesterol."

"So, is this just a social visit?"

Tom took a tentative sip of his black coffee—too hot—and shook his head. "Ben, I have to talk to you about that Triplex locomotive that was stolen from Bill. I know you're not into modeling, but it just doesn't make sense that some methed-up drug head would know enough to ignore Bill's other locomotive, which was newer and shinier, leave an easy-to-grab boxed set, and happen to take the more valuable engine that was difficult to spot on a hard-to-reach shelf. I hate to admit it, but my heart tells me a model railroader committed the murder." Tom glanced at the booth behind them just to make sure a fellow modeler wasn't around. The two Spandex-clad women in the booth discussing the merits of yoga versus Pilates over yogurt parfaits ignored him.

Ben added some cream and a teaspoon of sugar into his refill and stirred it slowly. "I appreciate you telling me, Tom, but it's not really much to go on, is it? Besides, the State Police are handling the case now. I can't tell you details of an open investigation, but you do know that I'm doing my level best to help them catch this guy. What do you want me to do, ask to inspect every modeler's house from your club?"

"No, but that does give me an idea," Tom replied.

"Now Tom, don't go doing anything foolish. Remember the time you thought it would be a good idea to figure out some calculus equations by having my younger brother jump off the garage roof? I was grounded for a month after my father found out."

"Hey, the math was sound. How would I know that he would land on a clothesline and drag your mother's whole wash load into the mud? But this is different. It's not unusual for me to drop in on these guys, anyway. All I have to do is keep my eyes open. I guess I'll see you at the wake tonight." Tom got up and left before Ben could say anything else.

CHAPTER 5

There were already 30 cars in the Feeny Funeral Home parking lot when Tom drove into the lot that evening. He had to go up and down a couple of aisles before finding a spot to pull into. He wasn't surprised at the big showing. William Joseph Murphy had been a popular guy. He loved to harmlessly flirt with even the oldest female customer and always had a wisecrack for any male shopper as he dispensed mounds of ground beef from the meat counter in the Acme. Sure, his humor could be a bit crude, but that was what many of his friends liked about him. Tom had long suspected that Bill had gotten into model railroading just to have an excuse to disappear to the basement, away from the four women in his house.

He went to sign his name in the guestbook, hesitating for a second over whether he should include Claire's name. Tom knew she would be there if things were different. He signed it "Tom and Claire McCloud." He walked over to Annie and her three daughters in the front of the hall. The oldest girls, Elizabeth and Caitlin, were the spitting image of their mother, with red curly hair and a button nose. They were standing next to men that Tom guessed were their husbands. The youngest daughter, Daisy, had Bill's broad forehead and blue eyes. He hadn't seen Bill's children for a while and was surprised to realize that they were now women in their early to mid-30s.

"Hi, I'm Tom McCloud. I was a friend of your father's," he said, reintroducing himself to each of the sisters as he went down the line. "Please accept my deepest sympathy."

Elizabeth and Caitlin murmured thanks and introduced Tom to their husbands. Daisy looked dazed and seemed to be operating on autopilot. She just gave him a weak smile.

"I am so sorry for your loss, Annie," Tom said, clasping her hand when he reached Bill's widow at the end of the line.

"I know you are, Tom," Annie replied. She still was as pretty as she had been as a cheerleader in high school, but Bill's death had seemed to add new lines around her eyes and mouth overnight. Her eyes were rimmed in red from crying, but she was making a valiant effort to stay calm in front of all the guests.

Tom noticed most of the usual suspects of club members were in the room. Maybe now they were actually "suspects." One person he was surprised to see was Eddie Paxton. Eddie had been a train modeler as a preteen, but once he had hit high school and discovered girls and motorcycles, he lost all interest in the hobby. The teenaged Eddie had dropped out of high school and usually could be spotted hanging out in the Roadhouse parking lot, drinking beer out of paper bags with the rest of the local riff-raff. As part of his new "tough guy" persona, Eddie went out of his way to avoid any of the train modelers who had mentored him in his youth. Tom would occasionally see him riding his motorcycle around town but gave up waving at him when the waves were never returned. Tom wasn't sure what Eddie's connection to Bill might be. If he was involved somehow with Daisy, he wasn't showing her any support. Tom watched Eddie go over and whisper something in Annie's ear. She emphatically shook her head no and he slid out a side door.

When the line of sympathizers ended, Annie and her daughters took their seats. After a brief prayer service, Tom worked his way through the crowd to exit out the same side door he had seen Eddie use. Eddie was pacing up and down near his Harley motorcycle, smoking a cigarette, a black leather jacket stretched over his muscular build. Tom thought Eddie was getting a little long in the tooth to still be playing a rebel without a cause.

"Hello, Eddie."

Eddie seemed startled to see him.

"Oh, hello, Tom." He took one last long drag and ground out the butt with his boot-clad toe.

"I didn't know you had stayed friendly with Bill after you left the club."

"What? Oh, no. I work with Annie at the Shell. I just came to, you know, pay my respects."

Tom had forgotten that Annie had taken a part-time job at the Quik Chek attached to a Shell station once her youngest daughter had graduated from high school. Eddie had worked at the station on and off for years. He was a skilled mechanic, but after a while he would stumble in late with a hangover one time too many and the owner would fire him. Sooner or later, however, the owner would be desperate for a good mechanic and Eddie would come back, swear he had stopped drinking, beg for his old job back, and their uneasy dance would begin again.

"Are you waiting for somebody?"

Eddie gave a weak laugh. "No, it was just too depressing in there. I came out for some fresh air and a cigarette. Nice seeing you again, Tom." He put on his helmet, pulled his dirty blonde ponytail out the back, and got on the bike.

"You, too, Eddie. You're still welcome down at the club anytime."

Eddie revved his engine, gave a brief wave, and rode off.

Tom saw about five butts strewn about the ground. It seemed like an awfully long cigarette break, even for an aimless person like Eddie.

CHAPTER 6

The day of Bill's funeral was sunless and cold with the threat of snow in the air. Men from Bill's extended family whom Tom had seen at the wake but hadn't had a chance to meet served as the pallbearers. One of them was his older brother, Hank. Hank's twin sons were there. All of them shared Bill's big frame and a ruddy complexion that was even more pronounced under the strain of carrying the casket. Tom and some other friends from the modelers' club took seats in the rear of the church. James and Emily sat to his right. He knew Gordon couldn't come because Donnie would never have tolerated sitting still in an unfamiliar place filled with people he didn't know.

Bill's boss from Acme got up and said a few words. His story about the time one of his elderly regulars got the wrong idea about Bill's attention and tried to trap him in the meat locker got a big laugh.

Then James talked about Bill's devotion to the hobby and how he had faithfully worked on the Christmas display each year. "The club certainly won't be the same without him," he said with a trembling voice. Tom couldn't tell if

James was distraught or giving an Oscar-worthy performance for the audience.

As he listened to the service, Tom had a strange sensation that someone was staring at the back of his head. When he spun around, everyone was absorbed in the service except a man furiously chewing gum who was engrossed in his cell phone. He did not seem to be paying attention to either Tom or the service. Tom knew he shouldn't be surprised that people felt compelled to check their messages, even at a serious occasion such as a funeral. Nobody else seemed to notice the man's rude behavior, but it still rubbed Tom the wrong way. When Tom passed the row on the way out of the church, the man was gone. Tom hoped it wasn't a reporter trying to get a scoop on the murder. So far, his role in finding the body had stayed out of the papers. If the man was a reporter, he was an uncharacteristically shy one. Or maybe Tom had just imagined someone was scrutinizing him. Finding Bill's body had unnerved him on many levels.

The graveside service was brief. The snow at least held off until the casket had been lowered into the ground. The biting wind and big wet flakes sped up the exodus of the mourners to their cars. Annie and the girls lingered briefly at the grave, the snow creating a light frosting on their dark coats.

Tom stopped by the Good Shepherd on the way home to talk with Claire. He knew she didn't remember who Bill was, but she must have sensed the sadness in Tom's voice because she listened to him patiently. When she patted his arm afterwards and said everything would be okay, it was so much like the "old" Claire that he felt a bigger lump of pain in his throat than he ever felt at the funeral.

Now that Bill had been laid to rest and the church basement reopened, the club regrouped and found the will to run the Christmas display. Everyone in the club told each other that it was what Bill would have wanted. Seeing the church basement filled with flocks of children running from one end of the track to the other excitedly following the trains helped ease some of the images of the horrible crime scene that were always in the back of his mind. It didn't help with Tom's nightmares, though. He kept dreaming that Bill was tied to the middle of some track in mountains of thick rope, just like in an old-fashioned *Perils of Pauline* movie. A 2-8-8-2 engine was hurtling down the track, a horrific cloud of blood pouring out of its smokestack. Its tender was filled with corpses instead of coal, their battered arms and legs hanging over the sides. The fireman was shoveling them into the firebox at a frantic pace. In the dream, Tom was rooted in place, unable to move to help his friend no matter how hard he tried. He opened his mouth to scream, but no sound came out. Instead of a whistle, the train reverberated with the cries of a thousand tortured souls. Tom could see the glowing yellow eyes and eerie grin of the ghoulish engineer at the controls as the locomotive inexorably bore down on his friend. The speeding locomotive was almost on top of Bill when Tom awoke in a cold sweat. After having the same dream for four nights, it was getting to the point where he was afraid to go to sleep. He hoped finding the murderer would somehow give him peace.

CHAPTER 7

The long winding driveway up to James' house built up the anticipation for the Tudor-style mansion at the end. Tom circled the limestone fountain with a spouting nymph at the front of the house and parked his truck alongside an emerald green Porsche. He was about to ring the bell when James' wife Emily opened the door, a tennis racquet leaning against her shoulder. She flashed Tom a dazzling smile with perfect teeth that looked like the "after" picture in a dental services ad. Her white tennis outfit gleamed against her flawless tan. Emily was about 10 years younger than James. Tom knew that the Busy Bee crowd usually referred to her as "that trophy wife," not that she would ever set her elegant high heels inside the coffee shop. As far as Tom could tell, their marriage was a contented one. She was not one of those wives who objected to her husband's modeling obsession, as long as he didn't interfere with her shopping or tennis obsessions.

"Oh hi, Tom. Sorry, I'm on my way out and James is down at the car lot. Was he expecting you?"

"I just stopped by to pick up the Skil saw that James had borrowed. Do you mind waiting while I go into his studio to retrieve it?" James' modeling kingdom was set up in a separate studio that was the size of some modelers' apartments.

"I'm afraid I have an appointment with the pro at the club for some practice. The door's open. You can just go in and help yourself." She flashed another brilliant smile and headed over to the Porsche. Tom couldn't help noticing the way her snug tennis outfit set off her full breasts and long tan legs.

Tom didn't know if he was more embarrassed looking at another man's wife or entering the studio to snoop. It's not snooping, he reminded himself as he perused the five levels of shelving going around all the walls. "I'll just take a quick look around," he said, apologizing to an owner who wasn't there to assuage his guilt. He knew it was highly unlikely that the stolen Triple 8 would just be sitting out to be admired, but you never knew. Even as he searched for the stolen locomotive, he had to stop and take time to appreciate James' layout.

James modeled the Pennsylvania Railroad in the 1950s. His intricate layout was 33' wide × 22' deep. He showed the PRR running from Pittsburgh to Harrisburg. Standing inside the 9' wide indent between the two 12' sections, Tom could see a sharp horseshoe curve on the left winding around the coal fields. On his right, looking back toward the meticulously painted background of verdant hills rising to a robin blue sky, he admired the stone arch bridge over a realistic Susquehanna River with track that was supposed to be running toward Harrisburg. In front of that was the Enola Rail Yard, the world's largest freight yard during the 1950s. A series of 18 coal-filled gondolas was lined up on the six lines of track, patiently waiting to be hauled by James' stable of freight locomotives. When James and his three-man crew were operating the layout, the freight yard would be busy with a Baldwin T1 4-4-4-4, a PRR K4 4-6-2, and a Baldwin N2s 2-10-2 freight engine. He also ran a Baldwin DR-6-4-20 diesel passenger engine, known as a "Sharknose" because of its distinctive cab design. It took an operations crew, just like a prototypical railroad, to staff the DCC controls and keep the trains on a strict schedule that avoided possible collisions. James loved the monster steam locomotives, but he also wanted to model diesel engines, so he had settled on the transition era of the '50s so he could have both types of engines on his layout. As if his layout wasn't big enough already, James was getting ready to knock down one of the walls of his studio so he would have enough room to add a helix of track (a stacked series of continuous loops). This would allow for a more realistic "timetable"—trains going through the helix would give the illusion of spending time in Harrisburg, dropping off and picking up passengers, before heading back to Pittsburgh.

Tom tore his eyes away from the layout and looked around the neatly arranged shelves filled with valuable Lionel engines and rare brass diesels. James liked to collect the best. Except there was a hole in the shelf where Tom knew a green five-strip O Gauge GG-1 from 1956 in mint condition that was a fairly hard-to-find engine used to be displayed. Another missing engine. Could that somehow be connected to Bill's death? Tom was trying to puzzle that out when he heard the studio door open. He grabbed his borrowed saw and turned around to face James.

"What are you doing here?" James demanded.

"Sorry to intrude. I just wanted my saw back. You had mentioned you were done with it. Emily said I could come in and get it."

"You could have called me and I would have dropped it off," James said icily.

"You're right. I happened to be in the neighborhood. Sometimes us retired folks forget other people aren't home during the day," Tom finished off weakly.

"You've shown yourself in so you might as well just show yourself out." James dismissed him with a wave of his hand.

Tom let out a long sigh when he was back in his truck. He just wasn't cut out for detective work. But seeing a locomotive missing from James' collection *was* strange. He'd go home and check out possible sales sites and eBay. Even if he found it listed, that wouldn't answer the question of why a rich collector like James would be selling off part of his collection. James liked to brag about each item he added to his collection, delighting in the envy of modelers who didn't have his kind of money to spend on the hobby.

After returning home and taking Lady for a long walk, Tom searched the refrigerator for lunch fixings. He put together a fresh turkey sandwich on rye with sweet pickles and ruefully used up the last of the deli mustard, working his knife around the bottom of the jar to try to get out every last bit. He would have to do a better job of making shopping lists with Claire away.

Claire was more than "away." The wife he knew was truly gone. He wasn't sure he accepted the fact that she wasn't coming home again any better than Claire did. Tom poured himself a glass of ginger ale and sat down at the kitchen table to peruse an issue of *Railroad Model Craftsman* magazine he had been meaning to read. He eagerly plowed through the issue as he ate lunch. He was always amazed at the ingenuity of some of the layouts described.

"Lady, there is just too little time to make everything and definitely too little money to buy all of the new trains reviewed," he told her as she patiently waited at his feet for any bits of dropped lunch. She sat up and gave a short bark as if she agreed.

After reading about the history of the 50-foot boxcar, he went to the back of the magazine to check out the classified ads. Tom felt a growing excitement when he saw an ad for a GG-1 for sale that sounded just like James' missing model. The ad listed a Pennsville area phone number to contact.

That was one mystery solved. Well, kind of. It didn't explain why James would be selling one of his prized engines to begin with. This detective work was giving him a headache. He was an engineer, so he liked straightforward answers to questions.

"After I wash the dishes, I should go down to the basement and work on my plans for a new garden railroad for a while. Maybe working with my hands will give the questions a chance to percolate in the back of my brain," he told Lady.

Claire had loved puttering in their garden. As she had lost the ability to finish a book and found going out with her friends to movies or lunch too confusing, she still took pleasure in working the soil and smelling the flowers. She had been the one to suggest that maybe Tom could put together a garden railroad. The large "G" scale models used in garden railroading were not something that Tom had been interested in before, but he had jumped on the idea of doing a joint project with Claire. Even though Claire would not now be able to run the railroad with him, he felt close to her while working on garden planning ideas.

Claire had planted the perennials according to a plan they had agreed on before she got sick. It was up to Tom to finish the rest of the track layout that would loop around the yard. He had found a plan in *Garden Railways* magazine for creating a bridge out of Styrofoam that could be painted to mimic stone. It would be perfect for spanning a storm drain he needed to get his future railroad across. He found himself humming his favorite Simon and Garfunkel song, *Bridge Over Troubled Water*, as he worked on carefully measuring and cutting the layers of Styrofoam. While he concentrated on the project with Lady snoozing at his feet, murder, missing engines, and the mysterious actions of James thankfully faded to the recesses of his mind.

CHAPTER 8

Early the next morning, Tom visited the Busy Bee and slid into the booth across from Chief Taylor.

"People are going to think we're an item if this keeps up," the Chief said, barely looking up from his pancakes.

"I just wanted to keep you apprised of my progress on the case."

Ben pushed his plate away. "It's not your case, so you should not be reporting any progress, or anything else for that matter."

"Okay. But you might be interested to know that one of our leading citizens is so hard up for cash that he's selling off some of his prized collection," Tom whispered, leaning forward into the booth.

"And who might that be?"

"Aha, so you are interested. I might be willing to tell you if you buy me a cup of coffee."

The Chief shot him a disgusted look but put his hand up to get Molly's attention. Once Tom's coffee was poured and Ben's syrupy plate removed, Tom told the Chief about his visit to the Spencer home and his subsequent discovery of James' locomotive ad.

"Was he advertising the stolen locomotive?"

"No."

"Then I don't see how it proves anything. A guy's got a right to sell anything he wants to."

"If it wasn't a startled drug addict," Tom replied, "there has got to be a reason someone would murder Bill. Maybe Bill knew something about James' financial straits. I imagine the big housing development that James used to brag about must have taken a lot of money. If word got out about James having cash flow problems, I would think the banks or his partners would lose confidence."

"Great, that's all I need to do is piss off one of our leading citizens. If I'm lucky enough to stay on the force, I'll be busted back to the graveyard shift. Okay, I'll see if I can discreetly make some inquiries. Now if you don't mind, the one person in this booth who is actually a police officer is going back to work."

CHAPTER 9

While he was waiting for the Chief to get back to him about James, Tom decided it might be useful to see if Annie could provide any information that would shed light on a motive for Bill's murder. He also knew that Claire would have wanted to see how Annie was holding up after the funeral. One of the things he loved about his wife was her compassion for people in difficult situations. Tom normally would not have wanted to visit Annie on his own because he had no idea what to say to make her feel better. He pushed through his reluctance by telling himself that Annie, of all people, would want to help find Bill's killer. Tom saw a tan Honda parked in the driveway as he pulled up to the Murphy house. He almost kept going, but knew it was now or never that he spoke to Bill's widow. He had a freshly baked chocolate fudge cake that he had made following one of Claire's recipe cards. It was the first time he had baked a cake and it didn't turn out half bad, if he might say so himself. Of course the best part was licking the mixer's blades without Claire slapping his hand away.

The three-story house with faded white paint was framed by a pair of large oaks and the gutters

were overflowing with dried leaves. Maybe cleaning the gutters was something he could offer
to help Annie with. He balanced the Tupper-
ware box housing the cake with one hand as he
rang the doorbell and waited on the screened-
in porch. Tom was still hoping that nobody was
home even though Annie's supervisor at the
Shell had confirmed that today was her day off.

After what seemed an eternity of standing
on the porch, Annie opened the door. He could
hear the TV playing in the background. "Oh,
Tom," Annie said, "I wasn't expecting you." He
thrust the cake in Annie's direction.

"I know it's not much, but Claire always said
that if chocolate couldn't make a situation better, it certainly wouldn't make it worse." He felt
foolish as soon as the words came out of his
mouth, but Annie smiled.

"Why don't you come in and we'll try some
slices with coffee."

"You sure I'm not keeping you from anything?"

"I'd love to have the company. The girls are
back at their homes. I was at such loose ends
today that I was reduced to watching *I Love Lucy*
reruns."

He followed Annie through the living room
as she shut off the TV, past a mantel lined with
sympathy cards, and into her kitchen, with its
cheerful daisy-patterned wallpaper and yellow
curtains.

Annie put on a fresh pot of coffee and set out
two yellow-ringed plates and matching cups
and saucers. As she moved around the kitchen,
Tom felt a little pang thinking about how much

he missed having Claire bustling around their kitchen. He also knew Claire would know exactly how to comfort Annie, while he felt about as useful as a screen door on a submarine.

"Do you have somebody who can help you clean out the gutters?" he blurted out.

"Somebody? Why would I have somebody?"

"I'm sorry. I just meant the leaf-clogged gutters look like something you could use help with. Rain water can back up in them and cause damage. I would be happy to come over tomorrow and clean them out."

"Tom, that would be great. I never realized how many details Bill *did* take care of. I thought he just played with those damn trains when he wasn't at work. Sorry, I didn't mean anything personal about that."

They moved on to safer topics, talking about what various acquaintances from high school were now up to. With the last crumbs of their slices of cake eaten and the coffee cups finally empty, Tom knew he had to ask some unpleasant questions without unnecessarily upsetting Annie.

He stood next to her and started drying as Annie washed the two coffee cups and plates by hand.

"Annie, I noticed a lot of modelers at the wake. I wasn't surprised because I always knew Bill was one of our more popular club members. But did he ever tell you about not getting along with one of them?"

"Not getting along, what exactly do you mean by that?" She turned around to look him squarely in the face.

Tom felt himself blushing. "I'm not sure what I mean. I've just been wondering if maybe this wasn't such a random act. It won't mean anything to you, but he did have his valuable Triplex locomotive stolen."

"What in the world are you suggesting? You think someone Bill knew purposely followed him into that church just to hit him over the head with his toolbox and steal one of his toys? I can deal with some druggie doing this, but a friend . . ." her voice trailed off.

Now that Annie said the words out loud, Tom felt truly foolish. "I'm so sorry to upset you, Annie. I'm just trying to help."

"I think you better go now, Tom. I appreciate you stopping by, but I really don't want to talk about this. And I think you better hold off on the gutters."

Tom had thought that Annie would want to know the truth behind Bill's death. Now it seemed like the truth, whatever that turned out to be, could possibly bring her more pain.

CHAPTER 10

Tom realized he had to talk to Gordon to see if he knew anything relevant about Bill's death and the missing Triplex, but he couldn't think of a way of broaching the subject with him. He felt a lot more cautious since seeing Annie's reaction to his theory about Bill's death. Yet Tom needed to buy some Christmas presents for his 2-year-old grandson, Connor, who would be visiting soon with Tom's son and daughter-in-law, so he had a genuine reason to stop by Gordon's store.

Gordon had owned Pennsville Toy and Hobby Shop for almost 25 years. The shop was an institution on Main Street, right across from the Busy Bee. It was the only place to pick up modeling supplies in the surrounding area. The toy part helped pay the rent, although he had been hard hit when a Walmart opened within a 15-minute drive. He still had a loyal base of customers who appreciated his modeling knowledge and special way with children. Some of the children who had gotten their first toys at the store were now shopping for their children. Gordon had achieved a certain share of fame by winning several first-place awards at NMRA shows because of his fastidiously detailed scratch-built engines and incredibly realistic dioramas. Although he always kept an aw-shucks attitude about his awards, Gordon was a smart enough business-man to prominently display his winning proj-ects in the train section of the store, which was catnip to every modeler who went back there.

What was even more apparent than his pre-cise modeling skills was his unflinching devo-tion to his son Donnie. Donnie had been diag-nosed at age 2 as having autism. Like many other autistic children and adults, he was fas-cinated by trains. Part of the appeal was the trains' wheels going around and around. Chil-dren with autism often have a preoccupation with spinning toys. Also, there is a definite tax-onomy of the hundreds of types of train mod-els that appeal to people with autism's fixation on organization and details. Donnie attended a special school during the day, but the minute he ran off the school bus, he positioned himself at the front of the store where he could keep an eye on the small *Thomas & Friends* layout. While he had limited verbal communication skills, cus-tomers learned not to approach him or move things in "his" section of the store because he would become agitated. Donnie made it clear that these were his trains and his layout. There had been a couple of unpleasant incidents at the store as Donnie got older. He had inherited his mother's big frame. At age 16 and an impos-ing 6'1" that seemed even taller next to his slen-der 5'7" father, he didn't realize what a threaten-ing figure he now presented. Gordon had taken some courses in behavioral therapy aimed at in-dividuals with autism and had a reward system in place. The therapy allowed Gordon to better interact with his son, although communication was still frustrating.

Gordon's wife, Madge, had never had the patience to go to the classes. She had always felt that Gordon had failed her, and Donnie was just the latest in a long pattern of disappointments. Customers had avoided her sharp tongue and tried to always have Gordon wait on them, which only focused her sarcasm on the few sales interactions she did have. It seemed everybody in town, except Gordon, had known about her affair with a part-time salesman in the shop, Harvey Waite.

"Harvey is a real go-getter, unlike you," Madge had made a point of telling Gordon every chance she got.

Harvey was a good 15 years younger than Madge. His blindingly white teeth were accentuated by the sprayed-on tan of his glowingly gold skin and slicked-back black hair. He had a habit of running his tongue along his lips, which gave him a rather wolfish appearance. Harvey possessed a sixth sense for disappearing when there were boxes to unload and shelves that needed refilling. Harvey managed to hold on to his job not only because he had Madge wrapped around one of his manicured fingers, but also because he was one of those mythical salespeople who could sell ice cubes to Eskimos, especially if they were female Eskimos. Still, people were a little shocked when Madge actually abandoned her son and husband to run off with Harvey three years ago, purportedly to New York City. Rumors circulated that Harvey was involved in some kind of boiler room fake gold coin sales scheme that kept Madge and him on the move.

Once it was clear that his wife had left him for good, Gordon expanded the store into the backyard lot so he could enlarge the train section. This was something Madge would never have permitted him to do. She thought train modeling was for "losers" and had reminded Gordon of that often, even within earshot of customers. After the expansion, which was his one act of independence, Gordon had retreated into an even smaller world of just Donnie, work, and modeling. Claire had tried to coax him over for a barbecue or other casual gathering. With his typical manner of never saying "no" outright, he had always hemmed and hawed and come up with an excuse, until eventually Claire took the hint and stopped trying. Gordon did show up at every regular Central PA Model Railroad Club meeting because he had been bringing Donnie since he was a baby. It was almost impossible for Gordon to make any changes to their schedule since like most people with autism, sticking to a set routine was of the utmost importance to Donnie.

"Hello, Tom," Gordon said as soon as he spotted him in the store, filled with holiday shoppers. "I'll be with you in a minute."

"No rush. I'm going to browse the children's section for some grandson presents."

Gordon gave a small nod and went back to patiently showing a customer how to oil his new HO 4-4-0 steam locomotive.

Tom found himself, as usual, stopping to admire Gordon's award-winning Civil War diorama that depicted the town of Manassas before its famous eponymous First Battle. It was like watching a moment of history only shown in grainy black-and-white photographs come to life in full color and motion. Tom had once asked Gordon why he would model preparations for a battle that the Union had lost. Gordon told him that from a railroad history perspective it was a milestone event because it was the first time that troops were taken directly to a battle by train. Gordon also had a personal connection. His great-great-grandfather, a Union soldier, had lost a leg in the battle but luckily survived to continue his family line.

The 52" × 35" diorama was bustling with the movement of troops and war supplies being amassed and civilian commercial products shipping out on captured Baltimore & Ohio locomotives and miscellaneous rolling stock. There were artillery and cavalry troops on the march in scrupulously painted and detailed uniforms, right down to the correct unit insignia. The track flowed around trees and plants native to Northern Virginia and past dirt roads being beaten down by the cavalry's horses. Tom had seen this diorama dozens of times but still found new details to admire. This time he focused on the field hospital being set up at the town church with horse-drawn "ambulances" being readied for the upcoming bloodshed. Tom had read a lot of different ways of weathering buildings, but he could never figure out how Gordon had gotten these mid-19th century structures to look so authentic.

While in the train section, Tom checked out

a couple of new Walther's building kits Gordon had just gotten into stock that looked like fun. No, Tom, he gently chided himself, you're here to get Connor a toy, not a present for yourself. He did need some track cleaning pads, so he grabbed a package off a rack before heading over to the children's toy section.

Donnie was in his usual chair right by the Island of Sodor layout watching Thomas go around as intently at 4:00 pm as he had been at 3:00 pm and would be until Gordon closed the shop up at 6:00. Tom waved, but Donnie ignored him.

Since Connor was still too young for electric trains, Tom selected a wooden Thomas set and some colorful storybooks. Tom walked up to the register with his selections as Gordon was finishing up the sale of the 4-4-0.

"Is that all today, Tom?"

"Yes. Well, actually no." Tom hesitated a moment. "I also wanted to talk to you about Bill."

"I know, I know, such a shame. We're living in really scary times. Another 10 minutes and that could have been me or Donnie. Are the police any closer to finding the druggie who did it?"

"Well, that's the thing. I'm not so convinced that it was a druggie."

"What do you mean?"

Tom tried not to think about what a disaster his conversation with Annie had been. It was like that first swim of the season in a still ice-cold ocean. Some people like to wade in very slowly. He always jumped right in figuring it was better to be cold for a short period than stretch out the torture.

Tom picked up a demonstration mini Slinky from a rack on the counter near the register and let it sinuously roll from hand to hand. "What you don't know is that only Bill's Triplex was taken. Don't you think it is strange that some druggie stole that weathered locomotive and left the Polar Express set and the shiny new Consolidation behind?"

"Oh, I don't know, Tom. Who can tell what's going through the mind of a killer high on Lord knows what? He most likely panicked and grabbed whatever he saw."

"Yeah, you're probably right. It's just something that has been bothering me. Claire always said that I'm like a terrier holding onto a mailman's pants' leg when I find something that doesn't make sense. It made me a good engineer, though."

Gordon chuckled but then looked at his friend seriously, "So how is Claire doing? Please give her my best wishes."

"Oh, she's doing as well as can be expected." This had become Tom's standard answer to any well-wisher's questions. It was vague enough not to be lying about her steady deterioration but definite enough to preclude any other questions. "Thanks for asking about her." Tom paid for the presents and pads and left the store. He wished it would be as easy to clean up all the confusion around Bill's death as it would be to clean the residue off his track.

CHAPTER 11

Tom drove by the Murphy house the next morning with the intention of making amends for offending Annie by offering to clear the four inches of snow that had arrived overnight. Bill had always used a snowblower, so it wouldn't take long to do the driveway and walkway to the house. When he pulled up, he noticed the Shell Station's tow truck parked in the driveway. As he started going up to the house, he did not see any footprints in the snow leading from the frosted tow truck to the house. It sure looked like Annie had had company last night. The most obvious candidate was Eddie. They are both adults, even if one adult is much older than the other, Tom reminded himself. It certainly would help explain Eddie's anxious vigil at Bill's wake. Okay, they were both adults, but if their affair had started when Bill was alive, then that just put the accent on the "adult" in "adultery." Well, I can't go barging in on her now, Tom realized. As Tom retraced his steps to return to his truck, he took one last look back over his shoulder. He couldn't be sure if he saw one of the upstairs bedroom curtains move or not.

CHAPTER 12

Talking to everyone he could think of who might know something about the missing Triplex had not brought Tom any closer to discovering the killer. It might have worked for Lieutenant Columbo on the old TV show, but it wasn't working for him. Tom decided it was time to analyze the matter precisely and logically, as he would have tackled any thorny issue that came up at his old job at PennDOT. He did not have the white board he used for problem-solving at work, so he took a sheet of paper and drew three columns with his trusty mechanical pencil and a T square. Tom wasn't a Luddite, but when he needed to do thinking, he found that a pencil grasped in his hand was more motivating than a blank computer screen. He wrote headings across the columns: "person," "opportunity," and "need." He knew that in traditional "crime solving," the last column should be "motive," but he understood systems engineering, not psychology. In systems engineering, the first important step was to identify problems or needs. Only then could you find solutions.

The first person he listed was James. James knew Bill was going to be at the church that morning, so it would have been easy enough to get there a little earlier. "Need"? Well, maybe he was so hard up for money that he was willing to steal a model to sell. It seemed to Tom that there would be a lot of easier ways to make money, such as "cooking the books" at one of his businesses. Hey, it wasn't as difficult as he would have thought to start thinking like a criminal. He erased "theft for money" as a possible motive. However, if Bill knew about James' debts and was threatening to expose him, that could be a motive for murder. He wrote down "blackmail" with a question mark.

Next he created a row for "Gordon/Donnie." They had the same opportunity. It could have been an accident on Donnie's part if he felt threatened by Bill. Bill had a habit of playfully punching people in the arm when telling a joke. That simple action could have set Donnie off. Then Gordon would have felt compelled to cover up the murder to protect his son. Even if it had been an accident, Donnie could never have understood why he needed to go to police headquarters or be questioned. As a father, Tom understood the instinct Gordon had to shield his son. Or maybe Bill had teased Gordon one time too many about Madge leaving and Gordon just snapped. But Gordon had been ignoring Bill's jokes for years. Tom got up from the table and made himself a cup of coffee before proceeding. He needed some caffeine to think clearly, but he understood that it also served as a bit of a delaying action before he listed the next name.

He sat down with the steaming mug in front of him. Feeling somewhat guilty for even suspecting a grieving widow, he added Annie to the list. She knew where Bill was going that morning. Bill could have found out about Annie's infidelity and threatened divorce. After arguing at home, she could have gone to the church. Giving Annie the benefit of the doubt, Bill could have gotten a bit violent about the topic and Annie might have swung the toolbox in self-defense. Or maybe Annie was more cold-hearted than Tom could have ever imagined and she wanted to kill Bill to avoid the scandal and expense of a divorce. Bill probably had a nice pension, which she could have lost in a divorce case.

This all brought him to Eddie. He could easily copy the opportunity and motive listed for Annie and apply them with a slight twist to Eddie, with or without Annie's complicity. Annie could have mentioned in passing where Bill was going that morning, or Eddie could have just ridden by the church and noticed Bill's distinctive T-Bird in the parking lot. Eddie might have wanted to spare Annie all the humiliation of going through a messy divorce. Eddie could have been counting on Bill's insurance and pension to help him and Annie live happily ever after.

Tom put down his pencil and sighed. Lady came over and sympathetically nuzzled his leg. He scratched her behind her silky ears. All of these "needs" seemed implausible to him as a reason to take someone's life. These "suspects" could be a dead-end and there was a Person X with a motive Tom knew nothing about. Or maybe it *was* a desperate drug addict, but one who happened to know something about model trains. He had never really thought about that coincidence. All in all, he wasn't sure if this listing had helped or not. What he really needed was some actual evidence that directly linked the murderer to the crime. Whether he liked it or not, he would have to go back and talk to all the people on the list again and hope one of them revealed something this time. That also supposes I would recognize a subtle piece of evidence if it presented itself, Tom mused. Maybe someone will conveniently shout "I did it." Doesn't someone always do that in TV shows?

"Well, I know one need that can be resolved," he told Lady. "I need to visit my wife. Hold down the fort until I get back. And if you figure out who the murderer is while I am gone, please put a paw print next to his or her name."

CHAPTER 13

Any lingering doubts he had about Bill's murder were driven out of his mind as he concentrated on preparing the house for a visit from Doug, his daughter-in-law Stephanie, and his 2-year-old grandson Connor. Although he often Skyped with them at their home in the Phoenix suburbs, it never filled the void of having his family live so far away. Connor had become a huge Thomas the Tank Engine fan, much to Tom's delight. He knew Connor would be thrilled to see the Thomas and Toby engines from the series added to the large scale Christmas train set he traditionally ran around the Christmas tree. After putting clean sheets and fresh towels in Doug's old room, he went over the grocery list from Stephanie and made sure to stock up on everything she requested for Christmas dinner as well as Connor's favorite cereal.

Tom hadn't realized how empty the house had been until the three of them arrived from the airport on December 23rd. Tom swelled with pride embracing the confident, well-tanned man that was his son. Marriage, fatherhood, and a senior engineering job with Boeing defi-

nitely agreed with him. Stephanie's sun-streaked
honey-colored curls bounced around her shoulders as she knelt, struggling to get the coat off
her keyed-up son. Stephanie was a sought-after
private personal trainer, but Connor still gave
her a run for her money. After hugs and kisses
with his beloved Poppy, Connor dashed off in
search of his second favorite part of visiting,
Lady. Connor excitedly followed Lady around
the house. "Lay, lay," he cried. She patiently let
him use her as a pillow while she laid down on
the hooked rug in front of the fireplace in the
living room. Tom and Lady shared babysitting
duties while Doug and Stephanie went upstairs
to unpack and freshen up. If they were tired
after their flight, they perked up getting ready
for the expected tide of visitors. The McCloud
house traditionally had been a gathering point
for Doug's friends when he was growing up, and
Tom tried to keep up this practice, even now
without Claire at his side. Tom had already put
up the Christmas tree and strung it with white
lights. Doug went to work hanging garlands and
red velvet bows around the staircase and mantel. Tom and Stephanie put up the eclectic as-
sortment of ornaments that the family had col-
lected over the years. Stephanie loved the small
wooden locomotive with a "1" that had marked
Doug's first birthday. Connor "helped" by trying to decorate Lady. She shook off the tinsel to
Connor's chagrin. He forgot all about Lady once
Tom got the train set running around the tree.
Connor sat down, mesmerized.

"I have never seen him stay put in one spot for
so long," Stephanie said appreciatively. "I think

we'll have to set up a train at home so his poor mother can get some rest."

"It always works like a charm," Tom said, as he put out bowls of pretzels, crackers, chips, and salsa. He was pleased he had mastered the recipe for Claire's famed horseradish cheese dip, her traditional treat for holiday get-togethers. Tom knew she wouldn't have wanted to disappoint guests. Even the pleasure of being united with his son and family and the promise of a joyous holiday ahead of them did not fill up the hollow feeling he had being apart from his wife. Her illness was a looming shadow that threatened to block out all their happy memories together. He focused on their last truly merry Christmas together when they were planning on new ways of enjoying being "empty-nesters." They had talked about taking a cruise together that summer, just the two of them, to Alaska. Tom had always wanted to ride the famed White Pass & Yukon Railroad in Skagway.

The doorbell rang, snapping him out of his reverie. It was the beginning trickle of a flood of old friends of Doug's stopping by with their families. The house soon echoed with the happy shouts of children and Lady barking at each new arrival. The men sipped beers and jokingly compared growing bellies and receding hairlines. Their wives cornered Tom in the kitchen. They did their best to stuff him with lasagna and casseroles and tempt him with home-made desserts, knowing he was missing Claire. Just like every Christmas past, the children gathered around the tree, laughing each time the train came into view. Some of them had to be dragged away in tears when their parents were ready to leave.

After the last visitor had left, Doug and Stephanie plopped down on the couch, jet lag and the long day finally catching up with them. As soon as Stephanie snuggled Connor on her shoulder, he was sound asleep. Tom bustled around, cleaning up the debris of empty beer cans and scattered snacks.

"Dad, let us just put Connor to bed and we'll be back down to help you," Stephanie said, handing Connor to Doug as she slowly got up.

"Honestly, I'm good. Everything is already wrapped up and put away in the kitchen. You guys head up. I'm just going to give Lady her last walk of the day and then I'll be hitting the sack too."

"Thanks, Dad," Doug and Stephanie said in unison, each giving Tom a kiss. Tom gave the sleeping Connor a gentle kiss before they all trudged upstairs.

The next morning, Doug took Connor to visit Claire. Tom stayed behind to help Stephanie do some cooking. They didn't want to tax Claire with too many visitors.

Once Doug and Connor were gone, Stephanie put Tom to work peeling potatoes. It was pleasant working side by side at the kitchen table as Stephanie trimmed green beans. For a while they worked silently, both enjoying the quiet after yesterday's hectic festivities.

Stephanie covered the beans with a little water in a small pot to steam later. She rinsed some greens for a salad and left them to drain in the sink, but hesitated before slicing some cucumbers that were sitting on the butcher block cutting board.

"We were going to tell you later, once Connor was in bed, but now may be a better time to share the news. Connor is going to be getting a little brother in five months."

Tom almost peeled his finger in excitement. He went over and gave Stephanie a big hug. "That's wonderful news!"

"The thing is, Dad, we would really like you to move to Arizona to be near your grandchildren. There are some excellent nursing homes in the area that would be perfect for Mom. I know Doug and I have casually asked you to move to Phoenix before and you just brushed it off. I don't think you realize how much it would mean to him to have both of you closer."

Tom went over to the sink and concentrated on washing and then carefully drying the peeler. "I need to take some time and give this some serious thought."

"Of course. It's a big decision. But remember, the clock is ticking for your next grandchild."

As if on cue, the back door into the kitchen opened and Connor ran in, followed by Doug. Tom saw Stephanie and Doug exchange looks.

"Connor, why don't you come and take a nap with me?" his grandfather asked.

Tom winked at Stephanie, "I am SO sorry to back out of KP duty. I think I saw Doug volunteer to help."

"OK, I'll let you off the hook this time, Dad," Stephanie replied. "It is definitely Connor's nap time, and I would like to hear about their visit to Mom." Stephanie gave Connor a big hug and kiss. Tom took off the barbecuing apron he was wearing and handed it to Doug. Doug made a face, but dutifully put it on before disappearing into the bathroom to wash his hands.

When Tom led Connor out of the kitchen, he saw Doug and Stephanie's heads bent over the cutting board. They were either conspiring to get him to move or just working on the salad. It made Tom think of a joke from the '60s: "You'd be paranoid too if everyone was against you."

He was quietly backing out of the guestroom after reading Connor a story and getting him tucked into Doug's old crib when he ran into his son coming up the steps.

"You're just the person I want to see. Congratulations on the big news! I'm so happy for you and Steph."

"Dad, can we talk a minute?"

"Sure, but you know I still need some time on my own to think about a move. Steph already gave me a sales pitch, so I'm not sure what you can add."

Doug gestured for him to follow him into Tom's bedroom and closed the door.

"Uh-oh, this looks serious," Tom said, as he sat down in a pale blue wing chair close to the bed. Doug pulled over the small chair from in front of Claire's vanity to face him.

"It's not about a move, although I'm glad to hear you're thinking about it. When I was visiting with Mom, she mentioned something about you investigating a murder. I'm never sure how much of what she says these days is real, but this seems like a bizarre subject for her to make up. Is it true?"

Tom guiltily looked at his son. "*Investigating* is a strong word. I think I told you in passing that my friend Bill Murphy passed away. I am sure you met him at a past Christmas train display or one of the model club's open houses."

Doug nodded.

"Well, he was actually murdered." Tom didn't think he needed to add that he was the one to find Bill's body. "Although Ben has been close-lipped about the subject, from what I can tell, the Chief seems to think Bill was just at the wrong place at the wrong time while some druggie was trying to burglarize the church. I won't go into details, but I think he was killed by a model railroader, possibly someone I know. I talked to your mother about it while I thought she was asleep. You know I am used to sharing everything with her. I had no idea she was actually listening. She never said anything to me about it."

"What about Ben? Why isn't he doing his job?"

"It's actually in the hands of the State Police. He is assisting them in their investigation. I'm just acting as his eyes and ears in the modeling community. Ben doesn't have the know-how I do to ask the right questions and pick up on any possible clues related to the hobby."

"And maybe you're antagonizing a cold-blooded murderer in the process. I can't believe Ben is encouraging you to do something so dangerous and idiotic."

"You know, contrary to belief, I am not a doddering old fool," Tom said with a rising voice.

"Then don't act like one," Doug shouted.

They were both glaring at each other when they heard Connor crying in the next room, "Daddy! Why are you yelling?"

"It's okay, buddy. Daddy is right here."

Doug picked up Connor and wrapped him around his shoulder. He gently rocked back and forth, humming *Twinkle, Twinkle Little Star* until Connor's eyes closed. Doug whispered over Connor's head, "Sorry, Dad. It's just that we all need you more than ever. I can't bear the thought of you being in danger."

"Don't worry. I promise to be careful. We better get downstairs to finish helping with dinner before your wife sends out the posse for us. The real danger is keeping a hungry pregnant woman waiting."

CHAPTER 14

Christmas morning arrived bitter cold with wind chills in the teens. Stephanie was shivering and Doug didn't look very happy as they ran to their rental car to drive to church services. Only Connor, whom they had bundled in a hat, scarf, and mittens and then wrapped in a blanket for good measure, seemed nonplussed by the temperature.

"As much as I miss you and Mom, one of the things I don't miss about living here is this brutal weather," Doug grumbled as he belted Connor into his car seat next to Tom sitting in the back. Doug passed along a plaid wool blanket he had grabbed from the house to his grateful wife in the front seat. "Here, honey, use this until the car warms up."

"You wouldn't mind so much if we had a nice white Christmas for you to play in," Tom said to Connor. Last week's snow had melted into piles of dirty slush. "Next year you'll go sledding with Poppy," Tom promised. "We'll go whee, whee, whee down the hill." Connor laughed, although he had no idea what sledding was or what Tom was talking about.

When they returned home from church, Connor's parents went through the time-consuming process of removing the many layers from their bundled son. As soon as he could wiggle out of their grasp, the desert-raised child scampered off in search of Lady, happy to finally be free of the restrictive winter clothing. After polishing off a lunch of delicious leftover turkey and all the fixings, the family finally sat down to open the presents stacked under the tree. Connor squealed with delight after unwrapping the wooden Thomas Railway and storybooks from Poppy and Nana and additional presents from his parents. Tom was thrilled with the framed sample of Connor's finger-painting art and a hand-knitted scarf from Stephanie. Doug had given him a sweatshirt embellished with the message "Still Plays with Trains," which they had a good laugh about. Tom knew they couldn't take back bulky items in their luggage, so he had given his son and daughter-in-law gift cards to their favorite Phoenix restaurants and shops.

Tom looked around the wreckage of wrapping paper left on the living room floor, listened to Stephanie emptying out the dishwasher in the kitchen, and met Doug's eyes. While they both constantly missed Claire, her absence was an especially painful hole when the rest of the family was together at the holidays.

As if reading his mind, Doug said, "You made the right choice, Dad, putting Mom in the Good Shepherd. You know how much she had enjoyed being around Connor. This year, she barely acknowledged him."

"I know. I just miss her so much. I visit her every day, but you know it is not the same as . . ." his voice trailed off.

Doug nodded. Claire's early-onset Alzheimer's might be a familial variety, but there was no way of knowing because Claire had been adopted and never had access to her birth family's medical records. Doug could have been tested for the gene that would signal he was a candidate for the disease, but he chose not to. Tom didn't blame him.

They both sat staring into the flames in the living room fireplace until Connor dragged Tom down to the floor to play with his new wooden train set. Doug soon joined them and gave voice to each of the train characters. Tom punctuated Doug's stories with accurate chuffs and whistles. The giggling Connor drove any dark thoughts from the room.

It seemed harder than usual saying good-bye to Doug, Stephanie, and Connor before they left to drive back to the airport the next day. Tom promised he would seriously think about moving. He gave Stephanie an extra tight hug, gratified to feel her belly containing his future grandchild pressed against him.

CHAPTER 15

The week before New Year's found Tom back in his normal routine. Mercifully, the terrifying death train nightmares had faded. He volunteered with Meals on Wheels through his church and was cheerfully delivering hot meals to shut-ins three days a week. Tom marveled at how much housework he had to do, including basics like laundry and vacuuming, to keep up with just one person. He wished he had helped Claire more when they were both working full time, often using the excuse that she would just redo things her own way. Tom had a "honey-do" list his wife had prepared while her mind was still sharp. He dutifully worked through the list, checking off items such as fixing a squeaky step, donating old clothing, and repainting the guestroom.

But no matter how busy Tom kept, a small voice still broke in asking why Bill really had been killed. He knew it was his training as an engineer that came back to haunt him. He hated loose ends that didn't make sense. Ben insisted it remained an open case and that the State Police were diligently pursuing every lead. Rose and Ben had stopped by for their traditional

MURDER TO SCALE   69

holiday visit while Doug and family were still in town, but Ben had made it crystal clear he didn't want to discuss the murder in any way, shape, or form.

Although there was nothing new to report on the murder investigation, the story was still getting play from local newscasts. Nothing like indicating there was a homicidal maniac on the loose to keep people tuned to local broadcasts.

Tom wasn't sure if he should reveal his role in investigating the murder to his best friend from PennDOT, Percy Littleton. Percy was a tall African-American who maintained a ramrod posture from his days in the military. Only the glimpses of gray in his closely cropped hair gave away his age. After 25 years as head of the PennDOT IT Department, Percy had retired three years before Tom.

Percy's wife Hannah had passed away from breast cancer right before his retirement, but his large extended family of children, grandchildren, nieces, nephews, and cousins were usually at his house on any given Sunday during football season to watch Steeler games on his 72" high-definition TV. Percy managed to dispense an endless supply of his famous barbequed ribs, keep a running commentary on the game, and tease his children mercilessly, without missing a beat. The family cat, Bradshaw, had learned not to sit on anyone's lap during a game because people were always jumping up to high-five a score or yell at an official. Over their many years of friendship, Tom had urged Percy to take up model railroading as a hobby, to no avail. Percy insisted that the best way to relax was sitting by a lake with a fishing rod, some cold beers at his side. Each knew he would never convince the other that he had the superior hobby, but they had a lot of fun trying.

Percy was visiting a daughter who lived in Greensboro, North Carolina, at the time of the murder. As soon as he learned about it from someone at his church, he called Tom. Tom promised he would discuss it when they met for one of their regular walks.

Percy and Tom met often to walk five miles along the paved pathway on the edge of a park located about halfway between their neighborhoods. They met at least twice a month, no matter the weather, before going out for a beer. They told each other that the walks prevented the beer from accumulating in their guts. Percy's grandmother had died from Alzheimer's, and he was one of the few people that Tom felt could truly understand what he was going through with Claire.

Percy was doing warm-up exercises when Tom met him at the beginning of the path. It was a brisk but cloudless day. The weak afternoon sun didn't do much to take the edge off the chill as they walked.

"I knew I should have stayed in North Carolina," Percy groused, pulling up the hood of his thermal sweatshirt.

"Nah, you would get too soft down there without me keeping you in shape," Tom teased.

As they walked, they shared family news and tidbits about retirees and current workers from their old office. Tom was delighted to reveal that he was becoming a grandfather again.

Percy's daughter, who worked in IT for a major pharmaceutical company, had gotten a promotion. When they stopped about halfway to take some swallows from their water bottles, Tom knew Percy had been more than patient waiting to hear details about the murder. Tom told him about finding the body, but for some reason he couldn't quite explain, he didn't go into his premise about a model railroader being the killer or his subsequent investigations into his fellow hobbyists. Percy had a sharp, logical mind. It was one of the reasons they had become friends. After being berated by his son and not finding anything concrete to support his theory, Tom didn't want to lose the respect of one of his most trusted friends by telling him about a wild goose chase.

Percy, who had served with the Marines in Viet Nam, had seen enough death first-hand. "I know it must have been tough finding a friend like that," he said sympathetically. Tom just nodded. They walked the rest of the way back to their cars in the comfortable silence that is possible between old friends. After they met up at their favorite watering hole, the mood lightened as they toasted Tom's future grandson and Percy's daughter's promotion with a round of beer and a couple of plates of buffalo wings.

One of Tom's wings fell on his lap, leaving a fluorescent orange streak before it hit the floor. Dabbing at it with a wet napkin only turned the stain into a spreading blob.

"I can't trust a man who can't hold his liquor, or his wings," Percy laughed.

"I think I better get this cleaned up in the

men's room," Tom muttered as he slid off the bar stool.

When Tom opened the bathroom door, the person leaving looked vaguely familiar. He seemed to be paying more attention to unwrapping a stick of Juicy Fruit than to Tom. Before Tom even made it to the sink, he remembered where he had seen that person before. It was the man he had seen checking his phone at Bill's funeral, the gum chewer. Was it just a coincidence the man was in the bar or was this man following him? If he recognized Tom, he hadn't let on.

Tom raced out and frantically looked around the dimly lit bar, now filled with a boisterous after-work crowd wreathed in cigarette smoke. "Did you see him?" he asked Percy.

"See who?"

"Um, a white guy about my height, brownish hair."

"That describes half the men in here," Percy said skeptically.

Tom gave up. He was chasing a ghost. "Never mind," he told Percy. "I thought I saw someone I knew. The dim light in here must be playing tricks on my eyes."

"Well, I have to get going. You know you're getting old when one beer causes you to see things," Percy said, clapping Tom on the back. "You, my friend, need to go home and get some rest."

Tom stopped at the Good Shepherd to see his wife before heading home. He wished he had her agile mind to help him now. She had just finished dinner, so he wheeled her into one of the center's book-lined public rooms for their visit.

Tom couldn't be sure, but he felt that Claire looked more peaceful when she was surrounded by books, even though she didn't read anymore. Claire had devoured murder mysteries, from the tea cozies of Agatha Christie to the Navajo Police stories of Tony Hillerman. Tom preferred to relax with a tome of historical nonfiction. He couldn't see the appeal of "who-dunits," probably because he hated puzzles. He always wanted to solve roadblocks at work as logically as possible. It was maddening that Bill's murder wasn't like a mechanical problem that could be easily solved, such as a locomotive that kept derailing and could be put back on track with an adjustment of couplers.

CHAPTER 16

Tom was driving home from the Acme the next afternoon, debating whether to use the chicken he'd just purchased for a chicken parmesan or chicken stir fry dinner, when he passed a weathered sign advertising Spencer Towne Village. He passed the sign every time he went down the road and had ignored it after the first week it went up, over two years ago. On a whim, he made a U turn to take the road pointed to by the sign. He went past a Christmas tree farm with varying heights of fir trees and a small orchard with winter-bare branches before another sign pointed to a turnoff onto a gravel road. After driving a bumpy half mile, he came to the end of the road. He parked his truck on a small patch of crumbling asphalt and walked up to a chain link fence bristling with yellow "No Trespassing" signs. Fast food wrappers, plastic bags, and empty cigarette packs were wedged along the bottom of the fence. A big banner hung prominently between two trees showed a community of elegant Tudor-style houses nestled among pine trees, promising "spectacular country living, starting at $400,000." Out of the planned 20 houses, only two were completed. Four more had framework done and nothing else. He could see empty lots in the distance marked off with tattered red flags. A small bulldozer sat forlornly atop a pile of dirt. The only sounds were an overhead jet and the wind swirling around the trash.

James had started the development just as the housing bubble burst. Obviously whatever money he had sunk into the project would not be recouped any time soon. It only added insult to injury that James' jewelry store and car lot also had been hit by the recession. But even if James *was* under tremendous pressure for money, how could that be connected to Bill's murder? Bill was a butcher, not a banker. How would he have intimate knowledge of James' finances? Had James' wife Emily suddenly switched from ordering filet mignon to ground chuck at the Acme?

Tom looked up at the banner again. The contractor listed was H. Murphy and Sons. H. Murphy was Hank Murphy, Bill's older brother. As an engineer, Tom did not really believe in "coincidences." Claire had often chided him about seeing the world in terms of black-and-white facts. "Tom," she would sigh, "people do not act logically. That's what makes them people." In this case, Tom's gut was telling him that there had to be some connection. It was also growling, which told him it was time to leave and go home and cook dinner.

CHAPTER 17

Tom had only briefly talked to Hank and his wife at Bill's funeral to offer his condolences. Rita Murphy, who refused to go by her given name, Henrietta, long before she married her husband Henry, was a short, stout woman whose handshake was as firm as her husband's. Tom had not talked to their identical twin boys, Henry Jr. and Harry (the "Sons" part of the construction company), at the church. Bill had jokingly referred to them as the "hungry horde," marveling at how many pounds of hamburgers and grilled sausage they could go through at his family barbecues.

Tom decided to take a chance and drop by the construction company's main site first thing in the morning. It was about 45 minutes away, but he figured he could stop by the mall for some new underwear while he was in the area so the trip would not be a total waste of time. He lucked out on finding Hank in his trailer office rather than out on a job. Even sitting down across the plank balanced on two filing cabinets that served as Hank's desk, Hank seemed to tower over Tom. While he shared Bill's imposing build and ruddy complexion, Hank had none of his younger brother's easy-going manner and desire to schmooze. He was all business when he asked Tom what his visit was about.

"First, let me again offer my deepest sympathy over the loss of your brother."

Hank gave a curt nod.

Although he had rehearsed in his mind what he wanted to say, Tom still felt unsure about the best way to question someone who was mourning a brother. Tom took a deep breath to steady himself before speaking. "The thing is, Hank, I don't believe Bill's murder was a random act of violence. I think someone who knew Bill, possibly a fellow model railroader, was responsible for his death. I'm hoping you can help me with some information."

"If you know anything about his murder, shouldn't you be talking to the police rather than me? I had zero interest in Bill's hobby. It's a colossal waste of time and money for a grown man, if you ask me."

"Once I have a solid foundation of facts, I promise I will talk to the police."

Hank grunted, which Tom took as permission to continue.

"I stopped by the Spencer Towne Village site yesterday and saw that it's not going anywhere. Did you have any problems getting paid for your work by James Spencer?"

Hank's eyes narrowed. "What the hell does that have to do with anything?"

Tom swallowed hard. "If you said something about James' debt to Bill, Bill might have said something to James to upset him." Tom knew he was clutching at straws as soon as the words came out of his mouth. Then again, maybe it wasn't what Bill said, but how he said it, Tom thought to himself. James had an incredibly thin skin and Bill's "jokes" could sometimes have a cruel edge to them. And Bill liked nothing better than bringing down people that he thought were "too high and mighty."

"That lying piece of crap still owes me $175,000, if you must know. I might have bent Bill's ear about it over a couple of beers. What of it? Why would James have killed Bill over his debt to me? Besides, that son of a bitch did manage to scrape together $25,000 for me last month. That and the fact that it would cost me a small fortune to pursue this in court are the only reasons he's not in foreclosure right now."

"Honestly, I'm not sure if this information helps or not, but somehow all the pieces will fit together in a pattern that makes sense."

Hank stood up, indicating that their discussion was over. As he shook Tom's hand, he held it tightly in one of his giant mitts and looked Tom in the eye. "If you can help catch the bastard that killed my brother, I'll owe you one."

Tom drove away thinking it was much better to have Hank in his corner rather than against him. But their discussion had created more questions than answers. For instance, how did that $25,000 suddenly materialize? It certainly didn't come from selling a few extra locomotives, or even the stolen Triplex.

He hated shopping, but he forced himself to stop by the mall and visit the department store to stock up on underwear. With nobody to see him in his skivvies anymore, he was tempted to wear his current stock until they disintegrated.

While Claire might not be in their house anymore, she was still very much his wife and he didn't want to disappoint her. He knew she would have disapproved of him wearing holey briefs. After making his purchase and grabbing a cheeseburger and fries at the mall food court, he headed back to Pennsville. He had Meals on Wheels dinner delivery duty that night. He then made his evening visit to Claire at the Good Shepherd. It made him feel better to tell her that he had bought new underwear, even though she was a little confused that a "stranger" was discussing underwear purchases with her.

He went home, had a quick dinner of some leftover chicken parmesan and an apple, and headed down to the basement to lubricate the HO Thomas engine from the church layout and the large scale engines he ran around the Christmas tree. He had a regular schedule to make sure his locomotives were lubricated after every 24 hours of use. As his hands worked carefully squeezing the light gear oil into all the metal-on-metal working parts—too much was as bad as using too little—his mind went back over his questions about James. Why a sudden payout last month? Maybe the Spencer Jewelry Store had gotten a big influx of cash from pre-Christmas sales. Jewelry. December. He caught himself just before he squirted a big glop of oil. During the Christmas "open house," one of Doug's friends who lived in the same neighborhood as James and Emily had mentioned that the Spencers' house had been burglarized the day before. It was part of a general discussion about the supposedly rising crime rate in Pennsville and it had not made much of an impression on Tom at the time.

The Pennsville police blotter reports were printed in the free local weekly delivered to his doorstep. Luckily, he still had a couple of months' worth in his recycling pile. After digging through supermarket flyers and the current month's issues, he found the copy for the first week of December. Bingo. A burglary was reported at 5XX Montvale Drive, with over $75,000 worth of property taken. Tom was positive that that had to include jewelry. James certainly had enough connections in the jewelry business to sell the pieces to someone who maybe was not a professional fence but who would not ask questions about paying out cash for jewelry at rock bottom rates. James could then "double-dip" by making an insurance claim for the full retail price of the jewelry.

Maybe it was time to talk to Ben again.

CHAPTER 18

Although he visited the Busy Bee during Ben's normal morning "shift" there, the Chief was nowhere to be found. As Tom exited the cafe, a light snow was falling and had already coated car windows and the patches of grass near the curb. He almost missed the small piece of white paper tucked under the driver's side windshield wiper. He unfolded it to see a message printed in small neat capital letters: "IF YOU VALUE YOUR WIFE'S LIFE, YOU WILL MIND YOUR OWN BUSINESS AND STOP TALKING TO THE CHIEF." Tom's mouth went dry and he felt the blood pounding in his head. It seemed like everything was in slow motion. He turned his head to the right and saw a trio of teenage boys throwing snowballs at a group of giggling girls. He swung his head to the left and saw an elderly man with a scraggly beard in a torn Army coat rummaging through an open garbage can. Anyone could have walked, or even driven, down the busy street and slipped the note on his windshield without being observed.

Tom's breath came out in ragged gasps as he jumped into the truck. He pushed the note deep into his coat pocket and drove as quickly as he could on the slippery streets to Good Shepherd. He raced past the receptionist without saying hello and stabbed at the elevator button. He was ready to run up the steps just as the elevator doors finally opened. It seemed like it took an eternity to get to the third floor. He bounded out of the elevator and narrowly missed colliding with a resident in a pink robe slowly navigating the corridor with a walker.

He forced himself to slowly enter Claire's room so as not to alarm her. The room was empty. Tom's heart sank. As he spun around, he knocked down an aide with her arms full of clean sheets ready to make the bed. He apologized profusely as he picked the aide up, who had managed to keep the sheets from hitting the floor.

Tom croaked, "Where's Mrs. McCloud?"

"Mrs. McCloud is in the rec room. It is music day," the aide said in a Jamaican lilt. "You know how the residents just love . . ."

"Thank you, thank you," Tom broke in. He sprinted around two corridors to the rec room. Standing at the entrance, he anxiously scanned the room before he spotted Claire in the front row. She was happily bobbing to "I Wanna Hold Your Hand" being played on a guitar by a young volunteer singing with extra lung power for his mostly elderly audience. It was only then that Tom was able to take a deep breath. He decided not to disturb Claire and quietly slipped out of the room.

When he got back into his truck, he took the note out of his pocket and read it again. "Talking to the Chief" could mean anything. Was he getting close to the killer? Maybe he had just rattled a skeleton having nothing to do with Bill's murder that someone had preferred stay unrattled. The question was, should he show the note to Ben? Once it became an "official" police matter, Ben would undoubtedly stop discussing any new information with Tom. On the other hand, if he didn't say anything and something happened to Claire, he would never be able to forgive himself. Not that Ben would post an armed guard outside Claire's room based on a vague threat.

He put the note back into his coat pocket. Okay, he would no longer "run into" Ben in such a public place as the Busy Bee. Maybe that would buy him some time. The only way he could protect Claire was to put the killer behind bars. He had always wanted to find Bill's killer, but now it was personal.

"Did you have to pick under the bleachers of the high school football field in January to meet?" Ben groused when he met Tom a couple of hours later. It seemed more cramped under the bleachers than when they had met there as teenagers. The spot had lost none of its appeal to the current generation of smokers, as witnessed by the piles of cigarette butts littering the space. "And what was with the cryptic text that it was urgent to meet you in two hours where we sneaked our first cigarettes? Have you joined the CIA?"

Tom briefly explained about the note not to meet with the Chief anymore, leaving out the specific threat to Claire. Instead he said there was a vague warning to keep his nose out of other people's business.

"I'm not sure what the note is referring to or who would have reason to write it," Tom insisted.

"I did warn you to leave people alone. Obviously you bothered *someone*," Ben replied, stamping his feet to keep warm. "If the note doesn't worry you, why did you have to meet me right now?"

"Did you ever check if that burglary at the Spencer house in December could have been an inside job?"

"Why do you ask that?"

Tom described his visit to Hank Murphy and the sudden payment by James.

"So wait, you want me to accuse one of our leading businessmen of insurance fraud just because he paid someone some of the money he owed? Is this before or after I also accuse him of murdering Bill Murphy because Bill annoyed him with one of his jokes? You really are losing your marbles." As soon as he saw the flicker of pain in Tom's eyes, Ben regretted those last words. Ben knew that every time Tom forgot a name or couldn't recall a football play from one of their high school games, he was worried that he was experiencing the first symptoms of Alzheimer's disease.

"Alright. Alright. I'll see what I can find out. And it is only because that burglary seemed a bit too sophisticated to be done by one of our usual suspects or a passing druggie. The thief managed to bypass their burglar alarm system and knew exactly when to strike when James, Emily, and their housekeeper were out."

Tom decided to go out on a limb with one

more question. "I assume there were no finger-
prints or other physical evidence linking Bill's
murder to someone specific; otherwise, the police would have made an arrest by now. Am I
right to believe that?"

"You know I can't share that kind of information with you. But think about it, even though
that Saturday was a warm day for the end of December, would you be surprised if people were
wearing gloves?"

"Thanks, Ben. You know we're on the same
side here."

"That's what I keep telling myself."

Tom was deep in thought after his discussion with Ben when he noticed traffic slowing
down to a crawl on Main Street. Members of the
Pennsville Volunteer Firefighters Squad were
positioned at the four corners of the intersection of Main and Chestnut Streets next to signs
asking motorists to make donations into their
awaiting boots.

Tom had been a squad volunteer before Claire
had gotten ill. Several members of the modeling club were also volunteers. Tom thought the
worst part of volunteering had been standing
on the corner asking for donations. He liked the
camaraderie of working as a chef at the squad's
annual pancake breakfast, especially with Claire
as one of the waitresses. Although fundraising
was a grind, between the spring pancake breakfast, summer "boot" collection, and Halloween
party, the squad had always seemed to get by.
Maybe donations had fallen since the recession.

He rolled down his window when he reached
the intersection. "Hi, Dennis," Tom said as he

dropped a $20 bill into the black rubber boot. "How's it going?"

"Not too bad, considering most people are tapped out after the holidays."

"I *was* kind of wondering why you were out soliciting today. Isn't the boot collection usually July 4th weekend?"

"Yeah, but we seem to be a little short this year."

The driver behind him honked his horn impatiently.

"Sorry, I have to go. Good luck to you."

It's a shame such an essential group has to struggle for funding, Tom mused to himself. I'm sure with James as president, he'll think of a creative way to help the Firefighters Squad keep going. Tom smacked himself on the forehead. While he firmly believed that people were innocent until proven guilty, he couldn't suppress a suspicious question that had bubbled up from his unconscious. Was it a coincidence that James, who was in desperate financial straits, was president of an organization that was short of funds? Although Tom was no longer a volunteer, Claire's second cousin, Isabelle, still served as treasurer. He could talk with her. And maybe he should talk to the treasurer of the modeling club while he was at it.

Tom was mentally going through a possible list of other ways to check up on James without alerting him when he hit a pothole on Chestnut Street. Even with a somewhat mild winter so far, potholes had blossomed in a few key spots. Of course people with common sense knew enough to drive around them, Tom thought. He pulled over and got out of his truck. He cursed silently when he saw the bent rim on the right front tire. Well, now at least he had a valid reason to visit the Shell Station. He had been putting off having a discussion with Eddie. Eddie's relationship with Annie had nothing to do with Bill's murder, so why was it any of his business? But it was one more piece of the puzzle that had to be fitted in place.

Tom managed to drive the teeth-rattling two miles to the garage. A white sports car was up on a lift when he pulled into the small service station attached to the Quik Chek. He assumed the man in the oil-stained overalls underneath the lift intently examining the underside of the car with a work light was Eddie. He would have approached him, but ear-shattering heavy metal rock blasting out of a giant boom box on the side of the bay made conversation impossible.

The station manager, Art Birch, scurried over to greet Tom. He was one of those people who always looked ready to jump out of their skin, even under the calmest circumstances. "Well, it is pretty obvious why you're here," he yelled over the mind-numbing music. "Can you wait? Eddie is just finishing up with that muffler job. Sorry about that noise, but Eddie refuses to work without it."

"Sure. No problem. I appreciate you fitting me in," Tom shouted into Art's ear.

Tom could see Annie at one of the registers in the Quik Chek looking toward the gas station. He couldn't tell if she hadn't seen him or was purposely not acknowledging him. He decided it was better not to go in and find out.

On the other hand, with Eddie, there was no way to know if he was truly annoyed to see Tom or was just generally in a bad mood because of a hangover. He practically ripped the truck keys from Tom's hand and drove the truck onto a second lift without saying a word. His boss scowled at him, but evidently decided it wasn't worth a battle today over Eddie's lack of customer service skills. Art hurried away to help a hassled woman in a silver minivan filled with four fighting children use the air pump.

Whatever Eddie's mood, he expertly put a new wheel and tire on the truck. He wordlessly lowered the truck and just grunted at Tom's sincere thank-you. Eddie picked up a small clipboard holding receipts layered with carbon paper and wrote out "NEW WHEEL & TIRE. LABOR & PARTS, $135.00," ripped off the bottom customer copy, and handed it to Tom.

Tom noted the amount and reached for his wallet, but then stopped. He recognized the small neat capitals Eddie had just used to write up the bill. He had seen them before on the anonymous note.

Eddie saw the flicker of recognition in Tom's eyes and grabbed the customer copy back. He looked more like a scared child caught with his hand in the cookie jar than the macho persona he usually displayed.

"Eddie, why in the world would you threaten me?" Tom bellowed over the music.

Eddie looked around to make sure Art was not nearby and turned down the blaring music. He plopped down on a ripped vinyl sofa that served as the waiting area for garage customers and studied an oil stain on the floor like it held the answer. It evidently didn't because he didn't respond to Tom.

"Did you murder Bill?"

"What?" Eddie jerked his head up. "Why the hell would you think that?"

"So you could have Annie to yourself."

"Annie to myself?" Eddie snorted. "Then how would I have time to party with Molly?"

Tom was totally confused. "What does Molly have to do with this?"

"I like Annie and all, but she's not about to join me drinking and hanging out with my friends, is she? I mean, I wasn't about to turn her down when she came on to me, but Molly is my main squeeze. It's been a major bitch all along to make sure Molly doesn't know about Annie. Molly's been telling me that you've been discussing all kinds of private things with the Chief. I wanted you to stop talking to the Chief at the cafe in case you decided to talk to him about me and Annie. I know you know all about us. I saw you checking out Annie's house the day my truck was parked there."

"Wasn't that note a bit dramatic?"

"Man, you have no idea what Molly is like when she gets angry. Now this is drama, big time." He pulled back his bangs. "See that scar?" pointing to a jagged line on his upper forehead. "That's from when Molly hit me with a beer bottle because she thought I was flirting with the bartender at Frank's Roadhouse. I hate to think what she would do if she found out about Annie."

"I promise, Eddie, I will not discuss you and Annie with the Chief."

"In that case, you and your wife have nothing to worry about." He handed back the keys to the truck.

Tom had half a mind to tell Eddie that he would, however, discuss the authorship of the threatening note with the Chief, but he realized he should quit while he was ahead. He would have liked an apology, but that assurance was the best he was going to get out of Eddie. Once again, he wished he could get Claire's input. He thought of her as a human lie detector because she always seemed to sense when their son or her students were lying. At this point he wasn't sure if Eddie was just a two-timing Romeo afraid of both women in his life, or if it was all an act and quickly admitting to the note was a coldly calculated way to throw Tom off his murderous trail. And if the latter was true, it was a trail that could violently lead right to his helpless wife if he wasn't careful.

CHAPTER 19

When he got home, Tom decided he better go through the pile of mail he had been neglecting on the entranceway table. After sorting out his bills and the usual junk mail, he found a copy of the quarterly model railroad club newsletter, *Scale Mail*. Younger members derisively called it the *Snail Mail*, but older members preferred to receive paper copies rather than email. He quickly scanned through it until a notice caught his eye. Gordon was having one of his periodic clinics at his shop on the following Tuesday, "Grow a Forest: Creating Trees Quickly and Easily. $5.00 donation for supplies requested." Tom envied the beautiful layered forests that filled Gordon's layout. He always thought it must have taken infinite patience to create not only the realistic quality but also the sheer quantity of his trees. Now was his chance to find out Gordon's tree-making secrets plus maybe have an inconspicuous chat with him or any other modelers who showed up.

Tuesday was a clear, crisp day. Tom found himself whistling *I've Been Working on the Railroad* on the short drive to Pennsville Toy and Hobby Shop. A handful of men were milling about the back area of the shop filled with several long tables that served as the work space for Gordon's clinics. Donnie was nowhere to be seen. Tom remembered that Gordon purposely picked Tuesdays rather than weekends for his clinics not only as a way to draw shoppers in on a slow weekday but also because it guaranteed that Donnie would be at school. Tom recognized two local modelers; the other workshop participants introduced themselves as out-of-towners. Modelers were often willing to drive a couple of hours to the shop to have a clinic with an award-winning master.

Each modeler had been provided with a handful of 16-gauge stranded wire; a bamboo skewer; a margarine tub repurposed as a mixing bowl for the glue, water, dish soap, and fine sawdust that would be used to create the bark; a small paintbrush; a bottle of tacky glue; a pair of nipping pliers; a travel-size can of hairspray; a clothespin; and three baggies holding poly filler and coarse and fine ground foam.

"Welcome to this week's episode of *MacGyver*," one of the workshop participants quipped.

Gordon led them through the steps of winding the wire around the skewer and then spreading out and twisting together strands of wire to create the "branches" and "roots." After trimming the ends of the wire branches, they painted the sawdust mixture onto the "trunk" and branches. Because it was a workshop, Gordon had provided drying lamps to dry the trees quickly so they could apply a second coat of bark before lining up to air-spray their trees with grimy black paint. Gordon explained that they would be using the tacky glue to apply poly fill and then later using the coarse and fine foam to create the foliage. The hairspray helped keep the foam in place.

Tom followed Gordon's patient instructions and made a quite presentable oak tree. As he put it down on the table to admire, he bumped elbows with his neighbor on his right.

"Sorry, I'm a southpaw. That's the reason I moved the supplies to the opposite side of the work area. I should have stood at the end," his clinic neighbor said sheepishly.

"That's okay. My wife is left-handed, so I understand." Tom felt an urgent rumbling in his colon, probably from last night's chili. He knew he shouldn't be eating spicy food, but sometimes he couldn't resist. "Will you excuse me?" he asked the lefty. "Nature calls."

Unfortunately, the one customer bathroom was in use. Tom remembered there was an employee bathroom in the basement that Madge had let Claire use one time in an emergency. Well, this is getting to be an emergency too, he thought as he headed down the steps to the basement.

After using the facilities, he paused by Gordon's workshop on the way back. There were lines of locomotives ready to be repaired. On a separate table was a graveyard of old locomotives that Gordon had picked up cheaply at flea markets and was cannibalizing for hard-to-find parts. It was a tangle of chassis, wheel sets, and miscellaneous parts. If Gordon had stolen the Triple 8 and then taken it apart, it could be right under Tom's nose but he would be hard-pressed to spot it.

The section of the workshop where Gordon obviously worked on his personal projects was immaculate. Tom admired how everything was so neatly organized that Gordon had what he wanted at his fingertips. But something else struck him—all the tools were arranged to the left of the work space, the way a left-handed modeler, such as his neighbor upstairs, would arrange them. He also spotted a left-handed pair of scissors like the kind Claire used. Tom knew Gordon was right-handed. Why would his tools be arranged that way and why was there a left-handed pair of scissors in his personal workshop?

"Can I help you with something?" Gordon had suddenly materialized at Tom's elbow. Even though Tom was startled, he managed to not blurt out the question in his head.

"No, no, just admiring how neatly organized you keep your workshop. It's an inspiration for me to clean up my act. Thanks for the clinic. I really learned a lot today."

Was it Tom's imagination, or did Gordon's voice take on a sudden coolness as he thanked him for coming? His smile was certainly as broad as ever.

After putting his carefully wrapped tree on the truck passenger seat along with Gordon's handout of instructions so he could continue growing his forest at home later, Tom decided to visit Claire before heading home. He found it cleared his mind to talk to her, even when she couldn't reply. He walked a couple of doors down from Gordon's store to Pennsville's only gift shop, which had been one of Claire's haunts because it featured a gourmet chocolate counter. He asked for two of Claire's favorite truffles, dark chocolate with a hazelnut filling. A chocoholic friend of Claire's who was perpetually on a diet had once compared these ultra-rich truffles to martinis: One was not enough, but three were too many. As an engineer, he had never been inclined to "romantic" gestures like flowers or jewelry. Happily, chocolate was his best fallback position for almost every special occasion he used to celebrate with his wife.

Although he now knew that the note threatening Claire was just a bluff, he still felt anxious about her safety every time he went to visit her. He checked with the front receptionist. "Has anyone else been here to visit Claire recently?" The receptionist cocked her head to the side and wrinkled her brow in concentration. "No, not that I know of. Do you want me to check the weekend logs? You know I'm not here on Saturdays and Sundays."

"No, I don't want you to go through the bother. I was just curious if any of her old friends might still be stopping by." He knew her friends, especially her closest friends, found it too painful to see Claire in her current condition, but he didn't want the receptionist reading too much into his sudden interest in visitors.

Claire was propped up in bed and staring at a black-and-white movie on her TV when he came in. He couldn't tell if she was really watching it or not. She didn't say anything to him as he blocked her field of vision. When he opened the miniature box holding the truffles and handed it to her, her face lit up. He sat down on the guest chair to watch her eat. She seemed oblivious to him as she devoured the prize and licked her fingers. That pained him because Claire had always had impeccable manners and would never have licked her fingers, even of melted chocolate, in public. He wet a paper towel in the bathroom and gently wiped her fingers. She went back to staring at the TV and did not pay attention to him, even after he started talking.

"Claire, I just don't understand about those tools. But I am pretty sure that Gordon isn't the one using his workshop."

CHAPTER 20

Tom had arranged to meet Claire's cousin, Isabelle, at the Starbucks past the shopping mall. He hoped there would be fewer prying eyes there than somewhere in Pennsville proper.

"Over here, Tom," Isabelle shouted as soon as she spotted him entering the store. A tall, buxom woman dressed in a bright pink pantsuit with numerous bangles clanging on her arm as she waved, Isabelle was hard to miss.

Tom went over and greeted her with a warm hug, being careful not to muss her immaculately coifed crown of gray hair and to avoid her long, crimson-lacquered fingernails. After they both picked up their orders, Tom steered her to a small table in a niche of the busy coffee shop where the other coffee drinkers were bent over their phones or laptops. No one gave them a second glance.

"It's always good to see you, but what's with all the subterfuge? I think it's safe to assume you're not here to discuss the family."

Isabelle's somewhat garish appearance belied her conservative accountant background, and she studied Tom with shrewd eyes.

Tom scanned the shop for any familiar faces before answering.

"Isabelle, I don't want you to get in any trouble, but I know you're still treasurer for the Volunteer Firefighters Squad. Have you noticed any, um, irregularities with finances lately? Not that I'm suggesting you did anything wrong," he hastily added.

"No, but I'm not the only one who can sign checks for the department. The president also can. And that same president delayed the department's annual audit because he insisted that our traditional auditors were charging us too much money and he wanted a chance to put the process out to bid." Isabelle paused to take a sip of her gingerbread latte.

"You know I'm not one to gossip, but I heard from my hairdresser, whose son is a blackjack dealer at the Sands Casino in Bethlehem, that Emily Spencer is one of his most regular customers. Unfortunately, while she may be playing often, she is not playing well."

Tom knew that truth be told, Isabelle loved to gossip. Claire had made it a point to avoid getting cornered by her at family get-togethers. And how reliable was this second-hand—no, make that third-hand information about Emily having a gambling problem? It did seem to fit, however, with James having financial problems that he'd rather keep secret.

Tom did not want to share his murder theory with yet another person, let alone someone as talkative as Isabelle. He fiddled with his coffee stirrer as he tried to think of what to tell Claire's nosy cousin.

"The Firefighters Squad's president is also president of my model railroading club." He realized that both Isabelle and he were tiptoeing around James' name as if he was the "Person Who Shall Not be Named" from the Harry Potter series. "I just have a vague feeling that things may not be kosher with the club's finances. I wanted to feel out someone else to see if I am just imagining things or if I should be concerned. I promise I'll tell you if I learn anything concrete. In the meantime, I trust this discussion will go no further."

Isabelle seemed satisfied by that explanation. She smiled and made a zipping motion over her glossy pink lips. Just in case she was still curious, Tom mentioned that Stephanie was expecting. That got her talking about her grandchildren, which he knew was a subject dear to her heart. After sharing some photographs of them on her phone, she glanced at the time and announced she had to run to a doctor's appointment. "At my age, that seems to be where I'm always running." She gave Tom a jingling farewell squeeze. "Please give my best to Claire."

"I definitely will. Please send my regards to Butch."

As he watched her leave the shop, plowing through knots of customers like a powerful ice-cutter ship, he hoped he was not misplacing his trust in her discretion. Tom shuddered to think what would happen if details of his investigation were leaked to the killer.

CHAPTER 21

Ominous storm clouds were rolling in as Tom drove to the regularly scheduled monthly railroad club meeting that evening. The trees along the road were whipping in the rising wind. There were plenty of spaces left in the parking lot of the American Legion Post. This meeting was not as crowded as the one held after Bill's murder that had brought out the curious along with the regular attendees. Tom counted only a dozen or so people. Gordon and Donnie had taken up their usual positions in the last row, in the aisle seats closest to the door, where Donnie felt comfortable. When Gordon noticed Tom looking at them, he gave a friendly wave. Tom was delighted to see Ryan had returned and was sitting in the front row. If James was feeling unnerved by his precarious financial situation, he was not showing it as he ran the meeting as imperiously as ever.

The first item on the agenda was setting up a permanent model train exhibit at the Children's Hospital. This had been proposed before, but nobody had figured out a way to get around the cost of maintaining a G scale exhibit. G scale, also known as large scale, would be sturdier for curious children to explore, but the trains would be more expensive to buy and maintain. Also, they needed to set up a layout that ill children could run themselves, which would take a little tinkering. When the club had taken over a small layout and run a few HO trains, it drew children in the hospital playroom like a magnet. Tom remembered one boy who had excitedly followed a train around the track, dragging his IV pole behind him. Tom was not sure who had smiled more that day—the sick children or the club volunteers. The hospital communications director had recently received a donation for play equipment that she told James she was willing to put toward setting up and maintaining a permanent train exhibit.

Tom found himself raising his hand and volunteering to speak to Earl Stanley Winston III to discuss what the hospital exhibit would entail. Earl was the ex-president of the model train club and a G scale modeler. Originally from Kentucky, he was a retired college professor who had taught American history at Lehigh University. Earl sported a thick silver mane and flowing mustache. Combined with his honey-dripping drawl and courtly manner, it was easy to see why Earl was a popular choice for the role of a Rebel general in Civil War reenactments. Professor Emeritus Winston combined his love of 19th century American history and railroads by writing and lecturing on Abraham Lincoln's role in developing railroads.

Unfortunately, Earl and James had had a falling out over James' snobby attitude toward G scale trains, especially when they were run on outdoor layouts. James wasn't the only train modeler who looked down at garden railroading, but he took every opportunity he could to voice his disapproval. James and Earl hadn't talked to each other in more than five years. As a result, Earl no longer even belonged to the club that he had helped start.

Come to think of it, Tom mused, there was no love lost between Bill and Earl either. Earl would sharply criticize Bill's modeling projects if he felt they did not exactly match the prototype in some minute detail. In his mind, he was helping Bill hone his craft. Bill did not take kindly to what he felt was Earl's nit-picking. Earl had been a skillful HO scale modeler who held himself to the same exacting standards he applied to others before the onset of Parkinson's disease had made it difficult to work in the smaller scale. With his usual ridicule of a person's vulnerabilities that he passed off as humor, Bill had taken to calling Earl "Old Shaky" behind his back. He only called Earl that to his face once. The venomous look from Earl was enough to stop even a bull of a man like Bill dead in his tracks. Earl's polished veneer had split just long enough to reveal a glimpse of the powerful emotions boiling just below his carefully constructed surface. Were Earl's barely constrained anger and Bill's cruel taunts, precisely calibrated to pierce someone's pride, finally a lethal combination? Earl would have known that Bill was at the church that Saturday because it was the traditional day to set up the Christmas layout. He could have gone there to examine the Triplex and made some critical comments of the award-winning engine. Maybe Bill retaliated and said something so belittling that Earl's simmering rage had at long last erupted into violence. While Tom felt in his heart of hearts that the murder wasn't the act of a surprised thief, he didn't see it as a carefully planned act either. The Earl versus Bill scenario he had just developed in his mind would support a crime of passion theory. He was not sure, however, that Earl would be physically able at this stage of his Parkinson's disease to hit Bill with the toolbox and carry off the weighty Triplex. But then again, Tom had read news stories of mothers lifting cars off endangered toddlers, so maybe the anger-induced adrenaline racing through his veins had given Earl extra strength.

That's ridiculous, Tom told himself. Earl was a talker, not a fighter. Tom had always enjoyed listening to Earl's colorful stories about the history of railroading. He knew Earl would also be a fount of knowledge for the garden railroad Tom planned to construct this spring, although he would have to plan on setting aside a large block of time for the visit. Once the former professor's "fount" was turned on, it could be difficult to shut off the torrent of information that would flow forth about his favorite subject. Someone in the club had once said that if you asked Earl for the time, he would tell you how to build a watch. In reality, Earl was much more likely to talk someone to death than clobber him over the head.

At Tom's mention of tapping Earl as a resource, James had just sniffed. James' strategy was to pretend that Earl no longer existed. To comment on Tom's suggestion would mean acknowledging that Earl was still walking the earth. Tom knew that if after talking with Earl he brought back the information that would help create the hospital layout but never named the source, James would accept it. Working in a government agency and Claire's tutelage had made him a master diplomat when the need arose.

James quickly moved on to the other business at hand, which was organizing a club outing to the Virginia Museum of Transportation. The Museum had restored a famous Class J 4-8-4 locomotive, #611, and several members were anxious to see it.

After the formal meeting ended, Ryan approached Tom with a host of new questions. They sat down together and were soon in a deep discussion about the best track to buy. Ryan wasn't sure if he wanted track that came with roadbed or if he wanted flex track that would allow him to create a more varied layout but would have to be ballasted. While pointing out all the pros and cons of different types of track, Tom never noticed that all the other members, including James, Gordon, and Donnie, had already left. The Post's caretaker came in and told them he was closing up.

"Sorry I kept you," Ryan said. "Thanks again for your help."

"I enjoy these talks," Tom responded. "I'm looking forward to seeing your layout someday soon."

"You and me both," Ryan said, shaking his head and chuckling.

Tom and Ryan had just enough time to dash out to their vehicles and get in before the first drops of rain pinging off the truck's roof turned into a steady drumbeat. Once Ryan pulled out, Tom noticed there were still two cars left in the parking lot. If one belonged to the Post's caretaker, who did the other car belong to? The rain turned into a monsoon, with gusty winds carrying sheets of water sideways. Even with his windshield wipers going, it was raining too hard to make out a figure in the other car.

Tom did not have time to worry about a possible stalker who might or might not be a figment of his imagination. He had to leave quickly if he hoped to get home before the poorly drained roads in his neighborhood became flooded. Was it his imagination or did his brakes feel a little spongy as he backed out of the parking spot? He saw that the traffic light ahead was amber. He lightly stepped on the brake rather than trying to rush through the intersection. He pressed harder on the brake pedal, but the truck did not stop or even slow down. He braced himself for a crash as he drove right through the red light. Luckily, no other car came through the intersection. However, the truck started to pick up speed as he went down a small hill. Tom frantically pumped his brakes again. Nothing. Booming cannon shots of thunder were echoed by the explosive crackle of lightning. A surge of primal fear rose from the pit of his stomach, pouring adrenaline into his racing heart. Don't give into it, he urged himself. Breathe!

Tom had left downtown and the road was becoming more winding. His windshield wipers struggled to keep up with the torrential downpour as he fought to keep the truck under con-

trol. His speed was up to 60 miles per hour.
Tom knew there was a curve coming up that
was best taken at 35 miles per hour. There was
no choice—he made a sharp right turn into an
empty field. As the truck roughly bounced along
deep ruts, flashes of lightning revealed glimpses
of a dense row of trees at the end of the field. He
turned off the ignition but the truck kept rolling.
Was he five seconds away from impact? Three?
It was hard to judge the distance with his high
beams barely cutting through the pouring rain.
His brain was rattling around in his skull like
he had just gotten clocked at football practice.
Suddenly he remembered something Coach had
told them during a Drivers' Ed class: "If there is
a problem with your brakes and pumping them
does not work, apply the emergency brake."

Tom sent up a desperate prayer and yanked
the emergency brake. The truck skidded violently but finally rolled to a stop about five feet
from a sturdy oak. Way too close for comfort.
He sat for a few minutes, catching his breath.
He felt like he had just run a marathon. He sincerely thanked the man upstairs for not making
his wife a widow. As soon as he was finally able
to release the steering wheel from his death grip
and flex his fingers, Tom called AAA. In a shaky
voice, he requested a tow truck, giving direc-
tions to his unlikely location based on his GPS.
The tree he had made at the clinic had been
thrown around the cab and now rested on the
passenger-side floor. Judging from its battered
wrapping, the tree was destined for the trash
rather than a layout. Oh well, thought Tom, bet-

ter a damaged fake tree than a real oak splintered by his truck, with him smashed along with it.

It seemed like an eternity but only about 30 minutes passed before he saw the tow truck's headlights searching the field and finally pulling up to Tom's location. The driver jumped out wearing a hooded mackintosh and thick boots. Tom was so relieved to get help that he didn't mind the rain dripping off his cap and down his collar as he showed the driver his AAA card. Tom asked him to take his truck to the gas station on the other side of town rather than the closer Shell station where Eddie worked. Anyone with even a passing knowledge of auto mechanics, which was probably half the male population, could have tampered with his brakes, but why take a chance, Tom reasoned to himself. The driver explained that AAA only would pay for a tow to the closest station and that it would cost him $200 to go to another station.

"I understand," Tom assured him.

The tow truck operator shrugged. Why argue with someone stupid enough to drive around dark fields in the middle of a torrential thunderstorm? It takes all kinds, the driver thought to himself. "OK, just sign here. Can you get someone to pick you up from the station?"

Tom was not looking forward to getting Ben out of his nice dry house on a night like this. It was going to be even worse if he had to explain to Ben that he thought his brakes had been tampered with because he had been poking his nose where he shouldn't have. Tom wanted indisputable evidence of who was behind this attempt on his life before he got in deeper with Ben. He sighed and called Percy instead.

Percy showed up at the gas station 20 minutes after the tow driver brought Tom and his truck there. He had not even taken the time to change out of a saggy sweat suit, just throwing a jacket over it.

"Are you okay?" Percy asked.

"I'm fine. My truck has some issues, though."

"Trucks can be repaired. Now what the hell is going on?"

Tom knew he owed his friend an honest explanation of why he was being called out to rescue him in the middle of a stormy night. He briefly went through his theory of Bill's murder and his subsequent investigation leading up to tonight's near disaster in as logical a manner as he could. The more Tom talked, the deeper Percy's scowl got until he at last exploded.

"What were you thinking? Can't you see you're in way over your head?"

Tom was too tired, too cold, and just too miserable to argue with Percy. He sank down in his seat and pulled his soggy coat around him in a vain effort to keep his teeth from chattering.

When they got to Tom's house, Percy insisted on coming in with him and making sure the house was secure. The storm had spent its rage, and the dark clouds had moved on to reveal a full moon. The wet streets glistened in the moonlight. Nobody seemed to be lurking about in the shadows, waiting to see if Tom had survived. Percy volunteered to give Lady a brief walk while he checked out the surrounding area. Tom gratefully headed upstairs to a hot shower and dry pajamas. When he came back down wrapped in a warm robe, Percy had found a bottle of brandy and poured them both drinks.

"Don't think this drink is a peace offering. I'm still angry enough to spit. How could you get yourself into this situation? You have been foolish and incredibly selfish. What about the people who depend on you, like Claire and your son and grandchild? If one of the soldiers who served under me in Nam had endangered himself like this" . . . Percy trailed off. After a long moment, he took a big gulp of brandy and continued. "But since you seem too pig-headed to tell the police everything, which is what you *really* need to do, how can I help?" Percy asked.

"I wish I knew. But I really appreciate you making an offer. And from the bottom of my heart, thanks for everything tonight." Tom raised his glass of brandy. "To friendship."

"Better yet, to honesty between friends," Percy said, looking Tom right in the eye. Tom nodded. Percy took a final sip of his drink and headed back out into the stillness of the late night.

CHAPTER 22

The next morning Tom woke up to Lady licking his face and sunshine streaming through his bedroom blinds. He glanced over at the clock on his side table and was startled to see it was 8:30. As he pushed up to get out of bed, his arms felt like someone had tried to tear them out of their sockets. "That's what I get for gripping the steering wheel so tightly last night," he muttered to himself. On top of the sore muscles, he felt groggy after tossing and turning all night over whether to report the brake tampering incident to Ben. When he had finally fallen into a fitful sleep, the death train again roared into his dreams. This time he was the engineer and Claire was tied to the track in the path of the sinister locomotive. Tom pulled and pulled on the brakes, but the train wouldn't stop. He realized it was only a dream, but it echoed the reality that he had a wife bound not by rope but by a terrible disease and he was powerless to help her.

Tom forced himself to think about what he did have control over. He was waiting to hear definitively from the garage, but he was sure the brake fluid line had been cut. He still didn't have any evidence to link either his brakes or Bill's death to any of his suspects or even his mysterious stalker. Of course if the stalker was waiting in the parking lot and had *really* wanted to kill him, he could have followed Tom and forced him off the road, knowing his brakes wouldn't work. I guess that's a comforting thought, Tom tried to convince himself. As a child, he had not believed in the Easter Bunny or the Tooth Fairy and kept a skeptical attitude toward Santa Claus. Why was he now willing to blame everything on the boogey man?

Still, *somebody* out there wanted him to drop his investigation into Bill's murder and was willing to use any means necessary to stop him. He could either give up now and leave a murderer on the loose or face one of his problems head-on by confronting James about his finances. It was not something he would want to do without backup, preferably by pulling out the big guns. The problem was he didn't literally have any big guns, just a rifle he hadn't used since he was a teenager when he went deer hunting with his father. He mulled this over while taking Lady for her morning walk.

After showering and having a bowl of cereal and two cups of coffee, Tom felt clearer. "Don't take this personally, but I need a better guard dog than you, Lady." She solemnly regarded him with her big brown eyes.

Suddenly he snapped his fingers. He did know a couple of big dogs in the form of Hank and his two sons. Tom knew *he* would be intimidated if the three of them wanted to question him.

A mechanic from the garage called and told him it looked like his brake line had been cut.

Tom said that he tried to do some other repairs himself and must have accidentally cut the line. The mechanic sounded dubious of that explanation, but he promised that Tom's truck would be ready at 2:30. Tom asked his neighbor for a lift to the station to pick up his truck. After he drove his repaired truck home, Tom called Hank and explained what he needed Hank and his sons to do. Hank readily agreed. "Even if James didn't kill my brother, I'm happy to put that weasel on the hot seat."

Hank called James and asked him to come over and evaluate some locomotives he had supposedly inherited from Bill. Tom hoped this appeal to James' vanity as a train expert would overcome any suspicion James would have about Hank contacting him.

It must have worked because James appeared at Hank's house that afternoon at 4:00. However, he couldn't hide his surprise at seeing Tom there.

"Hank, why do you need Tom here? I thought you wanted *my* in-depth expertise." James glowered at Tom.

"I was just curious to see these locomotives. I'm only here as a bystander," Tom assured James. Tom was a little worried at how adept he was becoming at telling white lies.

Before James could protest again at Tom's presence, Rita ushered everyone into the living room and set out some iced tea and home-made chocolate chip cookies on the coffee table. That kept everybody's hands and mouths busy for a little while.

Any relaxation on James' part evaporated

when Henry Jr. and Harry showed up. They didn't say a word, but the two offensive linemen-sized brothers formed a solid wall standing behind their father.

"I guess this isn't about trains after all, is it?" James asked, glancing anxiously from Tom to Hank.

"No, it's actually about you. I know a lot of construction workers in the Volunteer Firefighters Squad who wouldn't be happy to hear that their organization is missing money. It would be better for you to tell us anything you know about that," Hank said menacingly.

To their astonishment, James burst into tears. "You're right; I have borrowed money from the squad. But I swear, I will pay every penny back. If you must know, it's because Emily is sick."

"Well, if you have such bad medical bills, there are ways to work out payment plans with the hospital or doctor's office. That's no excuse to steal," Hank growled.

James pulled out a silk handkerchief embroidered with his initials and wiped his eyes. "In some ways, I wish it was an illness that a doctor or hospital visit could cure. Emily's illness is compulsive gambling. I've been robbing Peter to pay Paul to put back the money she keeps draining from our bank accounts. Every time I do it, she swears up and down that she has quit gambling. The next night, she's back at the casino again. I'm at my wits' end."

"So, what—you killed Bill because he threatened to expose your secrets? Or did you want to sell the Triplex on the black market since it was once featured on the cover of *Model Railroader*?

I've heard there is a Japanese collector willing to pay a small fortune for famous scratch-built locomotives," Tom said.

James turned as white as his handkerchief. "Murder Bill?" He looked searchingly from Hank's grim visage to Tom's stern face as if waiting for them to smile at a joke. "That's crazy. Trust me, I would never do such a thing." James gave a wave of his hand with some of his usual imperiousness.

"Why in the world would we believe such a thieving, lying excuse for a man?" Hank snarled. You're the last person I would ever trust."

"You know you're not helping Emily by supplying her with money. You're an enabler," Henry Jr. said softly.

Hank was startled to hear his usually silent son speak.

"My friend Mike is an alcoholic. We covered for him when he came to football practice drunk. We thought that was what friends do, but it wasn't doing him any favors. It wasn't until his drunk driving caused a car accident that left his girlfriend paralyzed that he got help. Emily won't seek help until she really has to."

"I already cut up all her credit cards and took her name off our bank accounts. That just made her more desperate. After I found out she had pawned most of her jewelry, I faked the house burglary to cover for it. It also gave me just enough money to keep you at bay, Hank."

"Tom, I am not sure how you found out, but as far as I know, Bill never knew about Emily's gambling. You were at all the club meetings and planning for the Christmas display. You know that if Bill had any inkling of my troubles, he would have been making snide comments about it. He liked nothing better than pouring salt in wounds and scolding his victims for not having a sense of humor. He even once asked you how you were enjoying your bachelor lifestyle now that you put Claire away."

Tom winced at the memory of it.

"You can check. I never sold the Triplex to anyone. If I could have avoided it, I would never have sold my GG1 that you saw missing. It was like parting with a child."

"You need to go the police and confess your insurance fraud," Tom said. "And you need to work out a repayment plan for the Volunteer Firefighters. That should keep them from coming after you."

"And if I'm in prison, how am I going to pay back the money I owe?" James asked, anxiously running his hands through his curls.

"I don't know," said Tom. "But you and Emily need to figure things out. Now."

"I think you're getting off lightly," Hank grumbled. "If it was just up to me, I would report you to the police right now and have your ass hauled off to jail. As much as I would like that, you're right, you won't be able to pay off what you owe while you're in prison." Hank leaned forward until he was inches from James' face. "But if any evidence turns up that you were the one who murdered my brother, you'll wish you had gone to a nice safe prison."

Tom could almost hear the air leaking out of James' inflated ego as he absorbed Hank's warning. The big shot who had confidently arrived looked totally defeated when he abruptly left. Tom would have felt sorry for him, but he still was not sure whether James was the killer. Wounded animals, and people, are surprisingly dangerous when cornered.

CHAPTER 23

Tom decided to try the element of surprise with his visit to Professor Winston the next day. He did not really expect to see the missing Triplex proudly displayed in Earl's living room. On the other hand, he did not believe that someone with Earl's love of the hobby could wantonly destroy such a model train treasure, even if he had just murdered its creator.

The leaden skies matched Tom's mood as he made the 45-minute drive past thinning suburbs and a patchwork of farmland to the even less populated area where Earl lived. His investigations were raising more questions about Bill's death than answers. How he missed Claire's insights into people. He didn't appreciate how much she had helped him make sense of people's actions before she was ill. No matter what he discovered or didn't discover today, at least this visit would not be a waste of time. He would get useful information for creating the Children's Hospital layout and some hints for his own garden railroad. That thought gave him some hope as he pulled into Earl's long driveway. Earl lived in a lovingly restored two-story colonial house set back from the road and framed by several acres of forests. The property was fastidiously maintained, from the reclaimed stone walls encircling the land to the historically accurate windows and slate blue shutters. When he parked at the end of the long gravel driveway, Tom almost expected to see horses stabled in the garage instead of the red SUV visible through the garage windows.

Earl was someone Tom's mother would have called a "confirmed bachelor," which was often code for a gay man. Tom didn't care about Earl's personal life, but it was relevant if that had provided possible ammunition for Bill's jokes.

Tom had just raised the pineapple-shaped brass door knocker when Earl opened the door.

"Good morning, Tom. I heard your car approach. What an unexpected pleasure." Although Earl might not have been expecting company, he was neatly dressed in a crisp light blue shirt, khaki slacks, striped tie, and navy cardigan sweater.

"Hello, Earl. I'm sorry to just drop in like this, but I was in the area and decided to take a chance that you were home. Do you think you have the time to have a chat about garden railroading?"

"I would be delighted. Please come in. I'll grab a coat so I can show you my backyard layout. Then we can move inside to see the trains."

Tom entered a narrow foyer dominated by an imposing grandfather clock and a porcelain umbrella stand holding some elaborately carved walking sticks. Earl grabbed a camel hair coat out of the hallway closet and one of the sticks featuring a painted mallard head. Tom followed him through the house. He got a glimpse of the formal parlor decorated with antique colonial-style furniture and gilt-edged mirrors topped by eagles. Tom knew from one previous visit that there was a huge den lined with shelves bulging with Earl's most prized trains and railroading history books. He still found it a little jarring to move from the 18th century to the 21st when they passed through the ultra-modern kitchen and sunroom add-on to get to the back door. Earl's workshop was in a large shed in the yard.

Even though the ground was frozen solid and a few hardy dwarf evergreens were the only plants visible, Earl insisted on a tour of his "garden" railway. It gave him a chance to lecture Tom on the origins of garden railroading in Britain. While garden railroads had sprung up in the United States between the World Wars, they had a second growth spurt in this country in the 1960s. Earl waved his stick to point out where different plants would flourish in the spring.

"Over there are my wonderful *Lobelia erinus*. Of course I make generous use of *Sagina subulata* between some of the paving stones."

When Tom looked baffled, Earl translated the Latin names as trailing lobelia, flowers known for their colorful blooms, and Irish moss, respectively.

Almost 2,000 feet of track wove around his 2 acres, including a gracefully arched stone bridge over a large pond and several trestle bridges. Earl said that some friends were going to help move the ground-level track to raised beds to give him easier access.

"Too bad you are not seeing the pond with all the lily pads and koi. You will have to come back for my July open house."

After 30 minutes of tramping around the ice-covered ground with a stinging wind that the surrounding trees did nothing to block, Tom thought his face was so frozen that it would break into pieces if he sneezed. He blew on his hands and stamped his feet, but Earl did not seem to notice his discomfort. When Tom asked about what trains Earl ran on the railroad, Earl finally said, "Let's go inside and I will show you."

Luckily Earl's Southern hospitality at last kicked in and he insisted on first making Tom some coffee using his new imported Italian espresso machine. Tom impatiently listened as Earl pointed out in detail the machine's many features. It took all of Tom's willpower to keep from blurting out that he would enjoy drinking any beverage, even the sludge that passed for coffee at PennDOT, as long as it was *hot* and served quickly. As Tom watched Earl grind the coffee beans and carefully measure milk for cappuccinos, Tom could see that Earl was left handed. Earl's tremors were less noticeable than Tom remembered, probably due to a more calibrated medicine regimen. Could Gordon have let Earl use his workshop before Earl's health problems? Perhaps Gordon and Earl both had enough of being victimized by Bill and joined forces to get their revenge by creating award-winning trains that would bypass anything Bill could make on his own. With Gordon's skills and Earl's encyclopedic historical and mechanical knowledge, they would make a formidable team. Maybe Bill had figured out that Gordon was hiding Earl's contributions and threatened to expose him.

Tom's thoughts were interrupted by Earl's instructions on the best Kona coffee beans to buy that somehow segued into the history of trains used on Hawaiian sugar plantations.

"Did you know that there were railroads on Kauai Island starting in 1881?" Earl said as he carefully carried the steaming cappuccinos to the breakfast nook table. Miraculously, only a little bit of coffee sloshed into the saucers when he put the cups down on the placemats with shaking hands. "Our very own Baldwin Locomotive Works, operating outside Philadelphia, was the main supplier to most Hawaiian plantations. The plantations preferred the 0-6-2 saddle tank engines, later referred to as 'Baldwin Bulldogs' because of their tractive ability and pulling power."

While Earl was temporarily distracted by setting imported Danish butter cookies on a delicate Wedgwood china plate, Tom took advantage of the slight pause in Earl's verbiage to ask him if he had heard about Bill's death and the theft of the Triplex.

Earl sat down heavily across from Tom. "While I do not wish anyone a premature death, I would be a liar if I said I was particularly upset by Bill's passing. The 2-8-8-8-2 was an amazing locomotive. You know the prototype was a beautiful Russia Iron blue. Baldwin Locomotive Works built three Triplexes between 1914 and 1916 for the Erie Railroad. It was built in an attempt to put a great deal of power in the hands of just one engineer. The engine made more sense on paper than in reality. Because of design flaws, only one more was ever built, for the Virginia Railway. For example, despite its huge boilers, the loco only produced enough steam to go 10 mph. Also, the rear engine's traction decreased as the boiler used coal and water, which lightened the tender."

Tom broke in, "But what do you know about Bill's scratch-built model?"

"I couldn't make the NMRA convention this year, so I never got to see it in person. I did see pictures of it, along with thousands of other people who saw it in *Model Railroader* magazine or online. Are you wondering if I saw it the day Bill was killed?"

Tom blushed. "As much as I hate to say it, I have reason to believe that a model railroader was Bill's murderer."

"One of my former students owns a pawn shop. I guess graduating with a history degree did not help his career path. Be that as it may, he had contacted me when the police alert went out regarding the Triplex because he knows I am an avid model railroader. That is how I learned the Triplex was missing. I am as anxious as you for the Triplex to be found. Although I find it hard to believe that such a stunning model was created by a morally repugnant piece of . . ." Earl stopped and smiled. "No, I am a gentleman. I will not sink to his level. But to answer your unspoken question, I was not at the church the day Bill was killed. I was doing research at the Civil War Museum in Philadelphia for my next book about the Lincoln funeral train. I know there were other books written about the Lincoln funeral train, but my book will be the most detailed one offered about the different locomotives used and the inside of the car that carried his and his son's coffins. You can check the research desk there, if you want."

Tom decided to take Earl at his word for now. It was already 10:30 and he wanted to get home in time for lunch. If he didn't get Earl to start discussing a large scale layout for the Children's Hospital as he had promised, he might not make it home for dinner.

Thankfully, Earl was happy to quickly sketch out a large scale layout for the Children's Hospital and promised to email Tom more details. Tom did have to spend another hour admiring Earl's 2-6-0 Mogul and hearing a detailed history about the engine before he could make his escape. Tom drove home dreaming about the garden railroad he would create. It was a pleasant change from obsessing about the possible snake in the grass who had betrayed Bill.

He was in his basement reviewing his garden railroad plans when the doorbell rang. When Tom opened the door, he was astonished to see Emily Spencer on his doorstep.

"I need to talk to you," she bellowed with undisguised anger. She did not wait for a reply before marching past Tom and into his hallway.

"Hello to you too, Emily," Tom said to the empty doorstep. He followed her into his living room. Lady was right beside him, eager to see who was visiting.

"To what do I owe this honor?" he asked, trying to lighten the mood.

She turned to Tom, her dark brown eyes flashing. "I want you to stay the hell away from my husband," Emily snapped.

Obviously this was not a social visit, or even a civil one.

"I'm not sure what you mean, but I see you're upset," Tom calmly replied. "Please, can't we sit down and discuss this?" he asked, pointing at a couch.

She ignored him and began anxiously pacing back and forth. "Don't play Mr. Innocent with me. I know about the confrontation you cooked up with that sneak, Hank Murphy. James came home and told me all about it. You need to stop sticking your nose into other people's business. I'm warning you," Emily said, approaching Tom while shaking her fist in his face.

That was too much hostility against her beloved owner for Lady. She crouched with her tail down and let out a series of sharp barks that turned into deep-throated growls. Emily glared at the dog but took a step back. Lady stood her ground in front of Tom but stopped growling.

Gone was the well-mannered, elegantly put-together Emily Tom knew. A madwoman had taken her place. Her usually sleek ponytail had been replaced by a rat's nest of frizzy hair. Emily's mascara was smudged and some of her hastily applied lipstick had missed her lips. Obviously the confrontation at Hank's house and the threat of prison had hit a nerve with James. He must have screwed up enough courage to lay down the law with Emily. Now she was in full panic mode and near the breaking point.

It was downright scary to face an addict who

felt backed into a corner. Tom was not sure how seriously to take her threat. He had a strange thought. Could Emily have been so hard up for cash that she killed Bill while trying to steal the Triplex? She knew James was meeting with Bill, Tom, and Gordon that Saturday. Even though Emily wasn't a modeler, she could have picked up enough knowledge just from living with James to know the Triplex was valuable. He knew Claire understood more about trains than she ever wanted to, just from being a dutiful wife and listening to Tom discuss his hobby.

"I'm not sorry that creep Bill is dead. He claimed to have caught me shoplifting a steak at Acme. It was just a misunderstanding. Bill took me back into a storeroom and tried to grope me. He said if I played nice with him, there was no reason to go to the police. Ha, like they would take his word against mine, the wife of one of the town's leading figures. I kneed him where it hurts and ran out. So you and Hank better call off that guy you had following me. If you think . . ."

"Huh? Wait, was this guy chewing a huge wad of gum?"

That out-of-the-blue question stopped Emily in mid-tirade. "I don't know. I didn't get a good look at him. But he got a good look at me, and it wasn't the usual once-over I get from men," she said, tossing her unruly mane. "I believe James when he says he doesn't know anything about anyone following me. He thinks I'm just paranoid. Of course I never told him about that incident with Bill. If Hank thinks he can get some

kind of evidence to use against James by following me, tell him I said he has another think coming. You are messing with the wrong woman."

With that she marched out as quickly as she
had stormed in. Tom heard the front door slam
behind her.

"Wow," Tom said as he sat down on the
couch. Lady came over and licked his face, trying to reassure herself that he was okay. "Thanks
for protecting me," he told her, scratching her
behind the ears. Despite seeing what Emily was
like when she felt threatened, he didn't think
Emily would have killed Bill over the storeroom
incident. James, on the other hand, was a different story. Maybe Bill had taunted James about
having a shoplifter for a wife. In his version of
things, Bill could have told James that Emily had
eagerly offered to exchange sex for silence, but
he had gallantly turned her down. James might
have just waited for an opportune time to get
his revenge. Tom knew that even he would have
wanted to throttle someone who insulted Claire.
He couldn't help wondering if his perceptive
wife had sensed the seamier side of her fellow
citizens. He was sorry he had to see it for himself. Life in Pennsville would never be the same.

CHAPTER 24

Two days after his visit to Earl and his encounter with Emily, Tom had just stepped out of his morning shower when the phone rang. He quickly wrapped a towel around his hips and rushed to grab the phone before the answering machine picked up. An early morning call could only bring bad news. Let it not be about Claire, he silently prayed before he recognized Ben's voice.

"Tom, I thought you would want to know that Eddie Paxton died early this morning in a motorcycle crash."

Tom had been so tense that it took a few seconds to absorb what Ben was talking about.

"Hello, Tom, are you there?"

"Yes. Sorry. What happened?"

"I wanted to personally tell you before you heard a garbled version through the grapevine so you didn't think this was part of your huge model railroading crime conspiracy. It was a deadly combination of booze, a motorcycle, and a curve. Honestly, with Eddie's DUI history, I'm surprised it didn't happen sooner. At least no other cars were involved. One of my officers saw some skid marks near that curve on River Street and found him under his overturned Harley. I'm waiting for confirmation, but the medical examiner's onsite impression was that it happened around 2:30 am. Eddie was seen leaving Frank's Roadhouse about 2:00, so that fits."

"Thanks for letting me know. Hey, I haven't had breakfast yet. Do you think I can meet you at the Busy Bee in about 20 minutes? I don't know if you knew that Eddie and Molly were seeing each other. You may want to gently break the news to her."

"Make it 45 minutes."

Molly's eyes were red and puffy and her hand shook as she poured their coffee. It was obvious she was not taking the news from Ben well.

Molly's eyes darted around the cafe. "Chief, can I talk to you a minute?"

"Do you want Tom to leave?"

"Eddie always liked and trusted Tom. I guess I can too."

Tom was embarrassed to be so publicly praised. He concentrated on stirring some sugar into his coffee.

"Oops," Molly said loudly, as she "accidentally" knocked over a small glass of water. She made a big show of grabbing some extra dishtowels to wipe it up.

"Hey, Mavis, can you keep an eye on things a minute while I clean this up?" Molly yelled at the woman behind the counter.

Molly leaned into the booth and began nervously drying off the Formica tabletop in small circles around their coffee cups. "I don't think Eddie's death was an accident," she whispered. "Eddie had been hinting last week that he was going to score a large pile of money. 'Babe, as soon as I get this dough, I'm taking you away from all this and we're going to start over in Cancun. We'll live like kings,'" Molly said, uncannily mimicking Eddie's voice.

"Eddie could talk a good talk and was forever promising me a better life, but this was different somehow. When I pressed him on it, he just smiled and said, 'Let's just say I heard something I shouldn't have and a certain someone will be happy to pay me the big bucks so I keep my mouth shut.'"

"And he never told you what he heard or who was going to pay him?" Chief Taylor asked.

Molly shook her head no.

"Okay, thanks for telling me. I'll let you know if anything turns up."

"You know, Eddie wasn't a bad guy if you got to know him. He did try to make me happy," Molly said as she brushed away the tears starting to flow down her cheeks. "Whatever or whoever he was mixed up with, he didn't deserve to die. For all his tough talk, Eddie wouldn't hurt a fly."

"Molly, these pancakes aren't going to walk to the customers themselves. You gotta pick up," the short order cook shouted as he stabbed an order slip onto the spindle by the pickup window.

"The way you cook pancakes, you can just bounce them over to their table."

That got some appreciative hoots from the counter coffee klatch. The cook slammed a plate of bacon down hard enough for a piece to slide off and disappeared back into the kitchen.

"Do you think she's telling the truth?" Tom asked, after Molly had gone to serve the pancakes, rubbery or not. "According to Eddie, she can be violently jealous. Maybe she forced him off the road and is telling us this whole story to throw us off track."

"What happened to the sensible engineer I knew who always liked to rely on facts?" Ben countered. "You're starting to see murder victims under every rock . . . or under every motorcycle. You think we have a homicidal modeler running around smashing friends over the head and following drunken motorcyclists around at 2:30 in the morning because he has nothing better to do. Until I see or hear differently, I am helping the State Police investigate a robbery gone bad that caused the death of Mr. Murphy. My report about Mr. Paxton's accident will be forwarded to PennDOT. They really should do something about that curve on River Street. This is not the first accident that has happened there."

Chief Taylor grabbed his hat, dropped some money on the table, and paused as he started to slide out of the booth. "But just in case your cockamamie theories are correct, that's all the more reason to stay out of this and let me do my job. I don't tell you how to play with your trains and you shouldn't tell me how to catch perps."

He left before Tom could think of any suitable reply.

CHAPTER 25

Tom decided it was time to update his original suspects list again. Writing things down usually helped sharpen his thinking. He added a row for Earl at the bottom after James, Gordon/Donnie, Annie, and Eddie. He only had Earl's word that he wasn't at the church that morning. If he had murdered Bill, Earl certainly wouldn't have admitted to Tom that he was at the crime scene. Under "need" he wrote, "avenging an insult." Maybe hitting someone with a toolbox was the modern equivalent of shooting an offender with a dueling pistol. Once Earl had committed one murder, was it such a stretch to get rid of someone who endangered the ex-professor's comfortable lifestyle? Trying to picture the threat from Earl's viewpoint, killing an amateur blackmailer who was as coarse as Eddie would be like squashing a buzzing fly.

Should Eddie still be on the list as a suspect for Bill's murder? Was it just a remarkable coincidence that Eddie died after hinting he was involved in a blackmailing scheme? If it wasn't an accident, Tom assumed that whoever killed Bill would be the same person who killed Eddie. But then again there were two jealous women who

unwittingly shared a motive for killing Eddie.
Either Molly or Annie could have easily figured
out that Eddie would be at the bar that night, followed him, and forced him off the road. Maybe
Annie was so traumatized from grief over Bill's
death that finding out that Eddie was cheating
on her was the straw that broke the emotional
camel's back. Eddie had shown Tom vivid evidence of Molly's temper. Maybe her story about
Eddie blackmailing someone was to provide
cover for her crime. But why stir the pot and
raise doubts when the police believed Eddie's
death was just an accident?

Speaking of women with tempers, maybe
he should add Emily to the suspect list. On the
other hand, why would she tell Tom about the
incident with Bill if she was trying to hide her
crime? Emily might be a lot of things, but she
wasn't stupid. If anything, as an addict leading
what amounted to a double life, she was profi-
cient at hiding secrets. He decided to leave her
name off the list.

What had he learned about his original suspects? Emily's gambling addiction on top of
James' considerable business debt from the recession meant James' back was up against the
wall. Bill had found out from Hank that James
owed him money. If James had arrived at the
church early that day, Bill could have joked
about telling the world that James' supposed financial empire was built on quicksand. Someone as self-important as James could have felt
compelled to silence Bill to preserve his image
as Pennsville's prime mover and shaker. Or now
there was the whole insulting Emily scenario to

consider, but Tom had absolutely no evidence that Bill had mentioned it to James. The more Tom thought about it, the more far-fetched it seemed that Bill would have brought it up. If anything, Bill wouldn't want *anyone* to know about what had happened, least of all Emily's husband.

He moved down the chart. Gordon was sharing his workshop with someone, possibly his good friend Earl. Perhaps Gordon had been there when Earl killed Bill in a fit of rage and Gordon was covering for him. Even more likely, Gordon was protecting Donnie because Donnie had violently lashed out after he had felt threatened by Bill in some way.

Tom crumbled up his chart and threw it away in frustration. Engineers worked from facts, not conjectures. There were still no facts that pointed directly to a suspect. Percy was right; he had no business trying to solve this case. Speaking of Percy, Tom guiltily realized he had not spoken to his friend since the night Percy had left his warm, dry house to come to his aid. Tom was about to call him when he was surprised to receive a text from Ben. "When ur right, ur right. Come to the police station ASAP." His call to Percy would have to wait. This message was too intriguing not to check out right away.

He drove as quickly as he dared to the modest two-story brick building that served as the Pennsville Police Station. A police dispatcher standing behind a bulletproof glass window seemed to be expecting him. He glanced at Tom's ID and escorted him right into the Chief's office. Ben was sitting comfortably with his feet up on his desk, his head tilted back and his eyes closed. Tom wasn't sure if Ben was sleeping or deep in thought. However, before Tom could even get a word out, Ben yanked his feet off the desk and sat upright in his big leather office chair. He pointed to an old wooden seat in front of his desk for Tom.

"Okay. I like to be right, but I have no idea what I'm right about," Tom said.

"We found that Triplex train you claim is linked to Bill Murphy's murder."

Tom leaned so far forward in the rickety chair he almost toppled over. "What? Where? Wait, the more important question is, with whom?"

That brought a smile to Ben. "Oh, you'll like this. It was in the possession of one Harvey Waite. Now isn't that a blast from the past."

"Harvey? That makes no sense. I never even heard he was back. And I thought there were no secrets in this town."

"We got an anonymous tip that Harvey was back in the area and that we would find something interesting in his car trunk regarding Bill Murphy's murder. That wouldn't be enough to get a search warrant, of course, but I told my officers to keep an eye out for Harvey. Sure enough, he was caught speeding in the canary yellow Camaro that's his pride and joy. When he was pulled over, he gave the officer permission to search the car. Lo and behold, there was the engine, wrapped pretty as a picture in bubble wrap."

"So why the glum expression, Ben?"

"It's a little too neatly wrapped up. Only a bow on top of Harvey was missing. Either Harvey is the greatest actor in the world or he was genuinely surprised to see the locomotive. When the officer told him it was evidence in a murder investigation, Harvey turned ghostly white under that fake tan and almost passed out. Plus, I don't like the idea of an anonymous call. When we traced the number, it was to a pay phone in the lobby of some fleabag hotel in Pittsburgh's Skid Row. According to the officer I sent out to investigate, there were no working security cameras in the lobby. The not-so-friendly desk clerk told him—wait, let me check my notes here—quote, I'm not paid to babysit the phone or harass our customers. I wouldn't care if Jesus Christ Almighty used it to order pizza, end quote. So anyone could have had access to it to make that call."

"Something else smells fishy," Tom interjected. "How would Harvey know the Triplex would be with Bill at the church? Bill was probably in the preliminary stage of building it when Harvey left town. I don't think Madge has been in touch with her husband since she took a powder, so she couldn't have found out about the Triplex from Gordon."

"It turns out Harvey has been lying low at his aunt's house in Lancaster for the last couple of months. That probably has something to do with the warrant we discovered from the NYPD in connection with some scam he was running up there. Our dear Harvey has a nice long record that includes several bunko schemes for ripping off older women. Most of the women declined to prosecute, but he did serve some time for grand larceny. He was caught trying to fence a diamond bracelet that he claimed one of his female admirers gave him. Madge is not in the picture. She probably figured out she gave up everything for a con artist and is too embarrassed to come back home. Harvey did not harm or even threaten any of his other victims, so I can't see him starting with Madge—no matter how big a pain in the ass she can be."

"But if Harvey did kill Bill for the Triplex, why was he driving around with it?" Tom added. "Harvey does not strike me as the sharpest crayon in the box, but he would be smart enough to at least hide evidence. Unless, of course, he was going directly to the FedEx office to ship the locomotive to an overseas buyer. I don't suppose he admitted to that."

"No, he lawyered up right away. But first things first. Besides giving you a chance to gloat, I called you down to the station for your model train expertise so you could verify that this is Bill's engine."

Ben took him to the closet-sized property room in the police station's basement. After putting on gloves, Tom was allowed to examine the engine. Although he had only seen pictures of it, there was no doubt in his mind that it was indeed Bill's scratch-built Triplex locomotive. The 2-8-8-8-2 was unquestionably a work of art, from its painstakingly inscribed builder's plates to the realistic tender truck safety chains to the rich Russia Iron blue color. It was a shame that a thing of such remarkable beauty could have been the cause of two hideous deaths.

"Ben, I can attest that this is Bill's one-of-a-kind engine."

"We will need you to put that in writing."

"No problem. Then what?"

The Chief rubbed his chin thoughtfully. "Well, we have enough to formally arrest him and charge him with grand larceny for possessing the Triplex, but not enough to charge him with murder at this point. Therefore, I don't have to turn him over to the State Police. We can hold him in the county jail until his arraignment. There's no question he's a flight risk. Even if the judge grants bail, I doubt he'll be able to make it, unless his aunt is stupid enough to mortgage her house. I would be willing to bet she doesn't know anything about her nephew's criminal past. Although it goes against all my instincts, I can't ignore this evidence. For now, I have to work on proving Harvey is Bill's murderer. Even if he's not, it's better that the real killer thinks the police believe the frame."

"I agree," Tom said.

"I think it's about time that you and I have a long talk about what you've really been up to," Ben told Tom. "Who have you been telling that the Triplex is the key to the murder besides me? And don't leave anybody out."

Tom knew he had to share whatever information he had. Maybe Ben could see a pattern he was missing. Tom went through his discussions with James, Gordon, Annie, Eddie, and Earl. He reluctantly told Ben about the affair between Annie and Eddie and Molly's jealousy. He talked about James' visit to Hank, including James' financial straits and Emily's gambling addiction. Tom briefly discussed Emily's angry visit, but left out her threat and her supposed shoplifting. Ben interrupted him once or twice with questions about the timing of Tom's visits. But if Tom's information made any light bulbs go off over Ben's head, he wasn't sharing that with Tom.

"Well, it seems that you've been a busy boy," Ben said when Tom was through with his narrative. "I appreciate your trying to help, but please let the professionals take it from here. If Harvey was framed, that shows the killer is getting desperate. There's no telling what he or she will do next."

That convinced Tom he was right in not telling the Chief about his truck's brake line being cut, because he was more determined than ever to keep investigating. He wasn't sure what Eddie's supposed accident had to do with anything. Ben hadn't revealed if there was any evidence, such as Eddie's Harley being tampered with, that made the police suspect that Eddie's death was not accidental. Tom knew if he told Ben that he had been in real danger from his investigation, Ben would make sure Tom stopped digging, even if he needed to post an officer at Tom's front door to stop him. Claire had always complained that Tom had an intractable stubborn streak. The more someone tried to throw him off track in this case, the more he wanted to get to the bottom of it. If anything, the incident with his brakes proved to Tom that he was getting tantalizingly close to the murderer. He just had to figure out exactly whose cage he had rattled.

CHAPTER 26

Tom desperately needed a distraction to clear his mind from dealing with this seemingly unsolvable mystery. Usually when he was mentally stuck, it helped to work with his hands. He couldn't do much more on his garden railroad until the spring. However, his interest had been sparked by his conversation with Earl on the Lincoln funeral train, which he had only a vague idea about. He was always eager to learn more about trains and history. From Internet research, he found out that the train, also known as the Lincoln Special, consisted of nine cars, one of which was built to be the President's car. Ironically, Lincoln never used it while he was alive. The car contained a parlor, sitting room, and sleeping compartment. There were 42 different locomotives used throughout the funeral trip. The somber train carrying the coffins of the slain president and his previously deceased youngest son, Willie, left Washington, DC on April 21, 1865 and arrived in Springfield, IL on May 3, 1865, after a few stops.

The most interesting thing he learned was that while there are drawings and some black and white photographs of the interior of the

Presidential car, there were no exact records of the colors of the exterior or interior of the car. A fire destroyed the train in 1911 while it was stored in Minneapolis, Minnesota. Tom distinctly remembered Earl bragging that his book would describe all aspects of the train in its full-color glory. Before Tom had left that day, the professor had told him that besides the National Archives, he had also done extensive research at the Civil War Museum, Union League, Historical Society of Pennsylvania, and Grand Army of the Republic Museum and Library in Philadelphia. Earl must have come across some unique material while he was researching his book, Tom mused.

"Boy, I would love to see some of that material before the book is published. I think a road trip is just what the doctor ordered," he told Lady. She wagged her tail enthusiastically. "Sorry, girl, this is not a trip you can come along on."

Tom did not get into Philadelphia often. Tom, Claire, Isabelle, and Butch used to make an annual pre-Christmas pilgrimage to Philadelphia when their children were young. Tom and Butch would take the kids to see the Wanamaker department store's light show and stroll through Dickens' Village at Strawbridge & Clothier. The piece de resistance was going to Reading Terminal Market to see the model train display while Claire and Isabelle did holiday shopping. They would all meet for a special lunch at Old Original Bookbinder's before heading home, the children fast asleep in the back seat.

It would be nice to visit Philly again at Christmastime, maybe with one of Isabelle's grandchildren, Tom thought. I could make an appointment to stop by some of the history museums and look at what Earl had researched.

"That's a great idea," Isabelle's voice boomed over the phone when Tom called her with his invitation. She dropped down to a whisper to tell Tom that James had come to her in private to confess that he had been "cooking" the Volunteer Firefighters Squad's books to cover Emily's gambling losses. "I don't know what you said to him, Tom, but he seemed sincerely repentant. I told him that the board would need to have an emergency meeting to deal with his embezzlement, but that I would put in a good word for him, especially since he voluntarily reported himself."

Tom heard a door shut in the background. "Hi, Butch. I'm talking to Tom," Isabelle said in her normally far-reaching voice. After a brief conversation with her husband, Isabelle said that they would be delighted to accept Tom's invitation and would want to bring along their 10-year-old grandson. Since they all couldn't squeeze into Tom's truck, Butch would drive them in his SUV.

Tom called the Civil War Museum on Pine Street in Center City, Philadelphia, to see if he could make an appointment to review Earl's research. While he was there, he hoped to find a way to check the sign-in book to verify the professor's alibi. The person who answered the phone said that the museum would be permanently closing soon, with its collection dispersed to Gettysburg and the Union League. That made Tom desperate to see the professor's research material while it was still accessible. He identified himself as a "colleague" of Professor Winston, which was only stretching the truth a tad, hoping that would help get him access. The museum volunteer hemmed and hawed a bit, but he finally agreed that Tom could stop by for an hour the following day and meet with the head archivist.

Butch agreed to pick him up early so Tom could make his 11:00 appointment. The more than 2-hour drive to Philadelphia the next day passed quickly as Butch, Isabelle, and Tom reminisced about their previous pre-holiday trips with their sons. Tom closed his eyes and saw Claire bent over the two boys wedged between them in the back seat, reading them a story. Butch and Isabelle's grandson, Kevin, had earphones on, his eyes fixed on the game he was playing on his smart phone. He had barely acknowledged Tom when he had been picked up.

They dropped off Tom at the Civil War Museum, which was only distinguished from the other attached houses on the block by a small sign in the window. They agreed to meet up at the Reading Terminal Market at 1:00 for lunch and to view the railroad display.

Instead of the mummified white-haired gentleman in tweeds that Tom expected, the archivist who met him for his appointment was an attractive middle-aged woman with coal black hair and emerald green eyes, dressed in a form-fitting gray sweater dress with tights and high-heeled leather boots. She had on a name tag reading "Caroline Trevors," but she introduced herself as Ms. Trevors. She insisted on calling

Tom "Mr. McCloud" and seemed a little miffed that he wasn't Professor McCloud. Apparently the ostensibly modern historian still believed in formalities. Ms. Trevors led him through the narrow museum, pausing to point out the stuffed and mounted head of "Old Baldy," General George G. Meade's favorite horse, gazing out from a wall. She seated Tom at a research desk and brought over the last box of items Professor Winston had signed for. Archive Box 1427.4 turned out to hold the effects of John Curtis Caldwell. It included several worn leather-clad journals or diaries of some kind.

"You know we don't usually let laypeople look at these, but since you are friend of the professor's, we decided to make an exception. Professor Winston is such a dear. He always brings me the most delicious cookies. Can I just see your driver's license, please?"

After verifying his identity, she returned his license and handed him a pair of cloth gloves.

"I must insist that you wear these and handle the pages with the utmost care. After all, these diaries are more than 100 years old. You can take notes, but no photographs. We also do not allow photocopying. Now if you'll excuse me. As you know, we are getting ready to close the museum and ship the collection, so we are quite busy."

A quick Internet search on his phone revealed that Caldwell had been a teacher, a Union general in the Civil War, a diplomat, and, most importantly, part of the honor guard on the Lincoln funeral train. Fortunately, General Caldwell had legible handwriting and orga-

nized entries, clearly delineated by dates. Tom
was thrilled to be touching something that connected him to a person who had lived in the
1860s. As much as he wanted to linger on the
mud-stained pages describing actual battles, he
skipped ahead to the entries on the days of the
funeral procession. April 20, 1865 was there, but
the pages for April 21–24 were missing. It looked
as if they had been neatly cut out using a box
cutter or X-ACTO knife.

When Tom called Ms. Trevors over, she
looked mystified. "I don't see how that is possible. No one is permitted to remove the diaries from the museum and only researchers
with permits are allowed to handle them. Let
me check the records again. She returned looking even more troubled. "Professor Winston was
definitely the last person to sign this box out, on
December 5th. It was signed out at 1:30 and returned at 3:30."

Tom considered the time period. Well that
puts some holes in Earl's alibi, Tom thought. Earl
would have had time to murder Bill by 9:00 and
drive to Philadelphia by 1:30. Tom didn't know
the exact time of death, but it couldn't have been
too long before he found the still-warm body.

Ms. Trevors had disappeared back to the library computer to confirm the exact contents of
1427.4. Along with the diaries, the box was supposed to contain a letter, signed by Mary Todd
Lincoln, thanking the general for his participa-
tion in the funeral train honor guard. There was
no letter in the box.

"Oh dear. I'll have to disturb the board president, who already started his Christmas break,

with this news," she said with a quivering voice. "He can talk to Professor Winston. I am sure they can sort it out."

"Yes, I'm sure he will want to discuss this with the professor before the police get involved."

"The police!" Ms. Trevors exclaimed.

She sat down, closed her eyes, and bowed her head between her trembling hands. Tom wasn't sure if she was meditating or praying. Whatever she did seemed to help. After a minute or so, she straightened up and once again looked her no-nonsense self.

"Yes, I'm sure you're right," she said wearily. "It's just that if we can't trust someone like Professor Winston, who can we trust?"

Tom did not have an easy answer for her. He glanced at his watch and realized he would have to hoof it to meet up with the family at Reading Terminal Market. Ms. Trevors would not let him leave, however, until she had confirmed his full contact information and got a signed statement. She quickly typed up a note describing how they had discovered the missing pages and letter and carefully watched Tom sign it. She told him to expect a phone call from the board president in the near future.

"I'm truly sorry, Ms. Trevors," Tom said. "Professor Winston is an old friend of mine. I don't want to think the worst of him either." He didn't tell her that thinking the worst would also include assuming Earl was a murderer as well as a thief.

Tom called Isabelle to let her know he would be a little late. He told her to go ahead and get their lunch and snag a table in the bustling market. Surprisingly, the disturbing discovery had not put a dent in his appetite. Maybe he was getting too accustomed to learning horrible secrets about people he thought he knew. After waiting in line for a cheese steak, he squeezed through the crowds to meet Isabelle and company at a table in the back of the market. Isabelle filled him in on their morning's activities while he ate the messy but delicious sandwich.

"So, how was the museum?" Butch asked, when he could finally get a word in edgewise.

"Interesting," was all Tom replied. Isabelle gave him one of her searching looks, but did not ask him to elaborate.

Now if he could just peel Kevin away from his phone, Tom was sure the boy would like the train display as much as his father and cousin had 15 years ago. Tom was grateful he had learned a few tricks from Claire along the way for dealing with recalcitrant children.

"Hey, Kevin," Tom said, touching the boy's arm to get his attention. Kevin's eyes had remained glued to his phone, even as he had finished up his lunch. "If you can stand being away from your grandmother for a couple of minutes, I've got something cool to show you. Of course if you'd rather hang out with your grandparents, I understand."

Kevin dragged himself along with Tom to the 500-square-foot model railroad display. Tom always marveled at the trains running on almost a third of a mile of track around a charming Christmas porcelain village. But within a couple of minutes of watching the Lionel trains go by, Kevin was excited too. He peppered Tom with questions and took some photographs. Tom knew that a seed had been planted. He could only hope that the hobby would take root someday down the line with Kevin.

When Isabelle and Butch showed up with a couple of bags of produce and Pennsylvania Dutch treats to take back, it was Kevin who asked for a few more minutes at the display. Tom winked at Kevin's grandparents over the absorbed child's head.

Then Tom's phone rang with an unknown number and he excused himself.

"Mr. Thomas McCloud?" asked an official-sounding voice.

"Speaking," Tom answered.

"This is Special Agent Flynn of the FBI's White Collar Crimes Unit. We need to go over your statement about Professor Winston. Where are you right now?"

The FBI? Why would they be involved in a theft from a Philadelphia museum? "I'm with my cousins at Reading Terminal Market. We're about to leave to drive back home to Pennsville."

"Stay put. I will meet you over there in 10 minutes. Look for a black sedan with government license plates near the Arch Street exit."

"What about my cousins and my ride home?"

"Your cousins are free to go. We'll make sure you have transportation home."

Tom gave Isabelle and Butch a thumbnail account of what had transpired at the Civil War Museum. He explained that he had no idea what the FBI wanted to talk to him about, but he really had no choice but to stay and answer their questions.

When Tom stepped out of the market's Arch Street exit, he walked over to a black car waiting at the curb. A tall, sober-looking man wearing a dark suit got out and approached him.

"Are you Mr. McCloud?" the man asked.

Tom nodded dumbly.

"I'm Special Agent Flynn." As Flynn flashed his FBI badge, Tom knew that once again his life had entered a real-life crime drama. They drove in silence the five blocks to the FBI's Philadelphia headquarters.

The agent led Tom to a small interrogation room with a folder and digital voice recorder on the table. Tom assumed that was a two-way mirror inset in the wall. Once they were seated and Tom had declined an offer of coffee, Flynn leafed through a folder that held Tom's statement to Ms. Trevors plus several other pages.

"OK. Let's get started," Flynn announced, pushing the folder to one side.

It dawned on Tom that the FBI had shown up with suspicious speed. "I know the FBI has a reputation of efficiency, and please don't take this the wrong way, but I'm surprised you responded so quickly to the theft report."

"Let's just say this is not the first time Professor Winston has been on our radar." The agent pressed a button on the voice recorder and began talking. "It is 15:30 hours. I am about to begin a session with Thomas Nicholas McCloud of 1 Ford Road, Pennsville, Pennsylvania."

"Mr. McCloud, you are willing to talk to us of your own free volition concerning any knowledge you might have regarding Earl Stanley Winston III, correct?"

"Yes, sir."

"Along with the recorder, I may be taking some notes. We appreciate your help. How long have you known Mr. Winston?"

Tom did a quick mental calculation. "I met Earl at the first Central PA Model Railroad Club meeting I attended, about 20 years ago."

"Do you socialize with him on a regular basis?"

"I wouldn't say I saw him on a regular basis since he left the club. When I visited him two days ago, that was the first time I had seen him in about a year."

"And what was the nature of your visit with him two days ago?"

"Can I tell you something off the record first before answering that question?"

Flynn shut off the recorder and shifted forward slightly in his seat. Tom took it as a signal that it was safe to continue.

"Is the FBI now involved with Bill Murphy's death? Is that why I'm here?"

A puzzled look passed over the agent's face before he quickly recovered his neutral expression. It was enough to tell Tom, however, that the FBI had not uncovered a connection between Bill's murder and Earl. Now he just had to find out what had drawn the feds to a library theft. Maybe Earl had tried to sell that Mary Todd Lincoln letter over state lines.

"Mr. McCloud, we'll ask the questions here." He turned the recorder back on.

"Again, what was the nature of your visit with him two days ago?"

Tom took a deep breath. "I went to see Professor Winston to discuss a large scale railroad for the Children's Hospital that our model train club is developing. He is no longer a member of the club, but we wanted to tap into his extensive knowledge regarding large scale railroads."

"Was that the only reason for your visit?"

"It was also to see if he might be a possible suspect in the murder of William Murphy."

"I do not see anything in your records indicating that you are a present or retired law officer. How are you involved in the investigation of that murder?"

Tom went over his discovery of Bill Murphy's body in the church basement, noticing that the Triple 8 was missing, and his theory that the murder was therefore connected to model railroading. He was careful to leave out any discussions he had with Chief Taylor.

"I see," said Special Agent Flynn. From the skeptical look on the fed's face, Tom wasn't convinced he really saw at all. "And how is this all connected to Mr. Winston, at least in your mind?"

When Tom described the professor's temper and the bad blood between him and the victim, Flynn at least took some notes. He was going to tell Flynn about the left-handed tools, but he figured he better quit while he was ahead, or at least while he still had some credibility as a rational person.

"I think I have everything I need. I'll be in touch if we need anything else. This interview has been concluded at 1600 hours." Flynn shut off the recorder and gathered his notes.

"But you still haven't explained why the FBI had Professor Winston on their radar to begin with or what is so interesting about a local library theft."

"No, I haven't," answered Flynn. He closed his notebook and stood up. "Special Agent Saxena will drive you home."

Tom always had problems converting military time like 1600, so he checked his watch. It was 4 o'clock, which meant he wouldn't get back home until after 6:00. Lady would be overdue for her walk and supper. He had been neglecting her far too frequently while he pursued all these wild goose chases. Why should she suffer because she had a nosy owner?

Tom called Percy. "Sorry, but I have been, um, unexpectedly detained in Philly. Can you please walk and feed Lady? You know where the spare key is hidden. There's dog food in the cabinet next to the fridge."

"Unexpectedly detained, huh. I know you're up to something related to the murder again, Tom. Tell you what. I'll take care of Lady as long as you tell me everything you've been up to as soon as you get home. I take it you can't talk now."

"That's right. Thanks again."

Special Agent Saxena turned out to be a young but grave-faced Indian-American woman. Tom was tempted to ask her why *every* FBI agent was a *special* agent, but he didn't think the solemn fed would find the question amusing.

After 20 minutes of driving in near silence, Tom cast about for a safe topic to discuss. He fell back on his standard icebreaker. "I was at Reading Terminal Market to see the model train layout. Do you like trains?"

The question brought a glimmer of a smile to the stern agent's face. "My grandfather was an engineer with Indian Railways. My whole family is interested in trains."

They spent the rest of the trip comparing the finer points of classic Indian and American steam locomotives.

Lady greeted him at the door, tail wagging vigorously, as if he had been gone for a week rather than just over 12 hours. After getting through the canine welcoming committee of one, he noticed the light was on in the den. Percy was camped out in Tom's leather recliner, reading the newspaper.

Percy looked up. "Ah, the prodigal son returns. I couldn't tell whether 'unexpectedly detained' meant you had been arrested for overstepping your bounds yet again, or you were kidnapped by the murderer and somehow escaped." Percy said it lightly, but Tom could detect an undercurrent of genuine concern.

Tom replied, "Did you eat yet?"

"Well, if you think pizza and a beer will help lessen the pain of listening to one of your crazy stories again, you're right."

Once a large pizza had been delivered and a couple of beers opened, Tom went through his eventful day, from the discovery of the missing historical pages from the Civil War Museum to his questioning by the FBI. "In my defense for missing Lady's walk, I might not have been jailed or even arrested, but I was detained." Tom paused to wipe some pizza sauce off his chin. "I still have no idea why the FBI was involved in a theft from the museum. But come to think of it,

I bet I know who does. If you're curious, stick around while I call the Civil War Museum's senior archivist. There can't be that many Caroline Trevors in the Philadelphia White Pages."

Ms. Trevors answered on the first ring, as if she had been sitting next to the phone, expecting a call. While Tom didn't think she had been waiting for his call, she didn't seem that surprised to hear from him.

"Ms. Trevors, I know it has been a hard day, and I apologize for calling you at home."

"That's okay. And after all we have been through, you can call me Caroline." Her voice sounded slightly slurred, as if she had been drinking.

"I assume you spoke to the FBI after I did," she continued. "If so, have they found out anything else about Professor Winston's thefts?"

Uh-oh, Tom thought to himself, she definitely said "thefts," plural. "Did you find other items missing from the museum?"

"Not from the Civil War Museum. As soon as you left, I made some calls to my counterparts at the Union League, Grand Army of the Republic Museum, and Historical Society of Pennsylvania. The world of historical archives is a small one, and we all know each other. Guess what? They each discovered historical material stolen from files researched by our mutual friend. The professor has been a very busy and very bad boy." There was a long pause while Tom waited patiently for her to continue. He heard some liquid splashing over clinking ice.

"One of them called his contact at the National Archives in Washington, DC. The pro-

fessor often discussed researching records of the
U.S. Military Railroads that are part of the records of the Office of the Quartermaster General.
That material is housed at the National Archives.
Sure enough, they are missing some documents
also. With all their security, no one is sure how
the professor pulled *that* theft off. But before you
could whistle Dixie, the FBI showed up at the
museum." There was another pause while Ms.
Trevors took a big gulp.

"I can't believe I was taken in by that smooth-
talking, cookie-baking thief. I trusted him completely. He's a historian, for Christ's sake," she
wailed.

"We all were fooled," Tom said soothingly.
"Please don't blame yourself."

"It's too late. It seems the museum board is
already blaming me. Now if you'll excuse me,
I'm really, really tired. Give me a call if you learn
anything else." She hung up before Tom could
offer any more words of support.

Tom filled Percy in on the half of the conversation he hadn't heard. "I'm not sure how these
thefts tie into Bill's murder. I can't believe Bill
knew about them."

"Don't jump to conclusions that just because Earl crossed the line in one area that he
was also a murderer. That's a much different
type of crime. And you are forgetting something
important."

"What's that?"

"I think it's fair to assume that the murderer
tried to kill you because you were getting too
close to him or her. Unless he's psychic, Earl
had no idea before today that you'd expose his

thefts. What would be his motive for cutting your brakes?"

"On the other hand, the thefts don't eliminate Earl from my suspect list either," Tom replied as he loaded their dishes into the dishwasher. "He was on my list to begin with because of his temper and the bad blood between him and Bill."

"Looks like you're back where you started from. I think that's my cue to head on home."

"Thanks again for taking care of Lady ... and listening to me."

"Your owner is crazy, Lady," Percy said while giving the dog a farewell behind-the-ears scratch. "He won't listen to my advice, so do your best to keep him out of trouble."

After Percy left, Lady ran over to Tom and solemnly put her head on his knee. "Are you offering protection or just hoping I saved you a piece of pizza crust?" He hoped her bark meant the former, but he knew it meant the latter.

CHAPTER 27

Tom flipped on the local morning news program on the countertop kitchen TV while he had his breakfast. There was nothing yet about an arrest of Earl.

Tom took Lady for an extra-long morning walk to clear his head and make up for his previous neglect. He had just returned home when his phone rang.

"Tom, this is Annie. I heard about Eddie," she said in a husky voice.

After seeing the way that Eddie's death had affected Molly, Tom had almost forgotten that Eddie had left two women, not just one, bereft. He fervently hoped Eddie was being cremated in a private ceremony. Having Molly and Annie, and Lord knows who else for that matter, grieving together at a funeral would not be healthy for anybody.

"Yes, Annie, it was a sad accident," Tom said, trying to keep his voice neutral.

"The thing is, Eddie told me to get in touch with you in case anything happened to him."

Tom dropped the end of the leash he was still holding. Lady let out a bark that seemed to say, "Hey stupid, aren't you forgetting about the other end?"

"Sorry, Annie, can you hold on a second while I unleash Lady? We just got back from a walk." He was grateful for the few seconds to get his thoughts together.

"OK. Now what exactly did Eddie tell you?"

"Well, the one day we were sort of snowed in together, he got kind of restless. He went downstairs into Bill's workshop to look at the train stuff that had been returned by the police. You know he was still like a kid when it came to trains. I wasn't too thrilled to have him go through Bill's things, but then I thought, Oh what the hell. Let him enjoy himself. I was sitting in the kitchen having a cup of coffee and could hear one of the trains running. It freaked me out because it sounded like Bill was down here. I hollered down the basement steps for him to knock it off."

"Eddie came up into the kitchen with a strange look on his face, sort of like the expression my cat has when she triumphantly drops a mouse at my feet."

"I asked him, 'What the hell got into you?'"

"He said, 'In case anything ever happens to me, tell Tom to look at Bill's Console'—or Consolation or Consolidation or something like that. 'And don't let ANYONE else down there.' I had no idea what he was talking about. Then he got restless again for something else and we went upstairs. I had completely forgotten about it until now."

"Annie, is it okay if I come over?"

"I think you'd better."

Tom compulsively checked his rear-view mirror as he drove over to Annie's house. Even though he didn't see anyone following him, he took a convoluted route to her house and parked a couple of blocks away.

Annie opened the door at his first knock, so she must have been waiting in the foyer for him. She opened the door just wide enough for him to enter and locked the deadbolt after he was in. The sunny kitchen he had previously visited looked ominously dark with only the stovetop overhead light on. A bottle of beer cast a long shadow on the table. She opened the basement door and turned on the overhead fluorescent lights. "I'm sorry about the mess. I just don't have the heart to clean up any of his things yet," she said, as she led the way down the narrow, steep steps.

Once he reached the bottom of the steps and entered Bill's workshop area, Tom was inescapably drawn to the colorful circus train that Bill had been working on. The heavyweight passenger cars and rolling stock were in various stages of being painted in 1940s to early 1950s *Ringling Bros. and Barnum & Bailey* paint schemes. It looked like this train was going to be pulled by a mighty Union Pacific 4-8-8-4 (the aptly nicknamed "Big Boy") steam locomotive, since circuses did not have their own engines. Bill had assembled a veritable ark's worth of lions, tigers, elephants, horses, camels, zebras, and giraffes. Some were being led down ramps from the 75' stock cars. The 75' flat cars were loaded with tent poles, trucks, tractors, a cannon for the human cannonball, a traditional steam calliope, and

other equipment needed for the set-up and operation of the "Greatest Show on Earth." Sheets
of prototypical decals Bill had printed out from
his computer and didn't have a chance to apply
lay scattered about.

"It's a shame Bill's life was cut short before
he could enjoy finishing this project. It was evidently a labor of love," Tom said. "I had almost
forgotten what a talented modeler Bill was."

Annie also was clearly fascinated by the scene,
crouching down to admire the details on the
dining car and coaches at eye level. "I should
have paid more attention to what Bill was doing
down here. I always made a beeline to the laundry area on the right and never stopped by his
work area," she confessed. "I had no idea he was
creating such an amazing project. Maybe if I
had admired his handiwork instead of resenting
the time he spent on it, things would have been
different between us," Annie said wistfully.

Tom tore himself away to look at Bill's small
oval of test track and saw the Consolidation sitting there. He picked it up and turned it over.
Nothing looked out of the ordinary to him. He
was foolishly hoping Bill had scrawled the killer's name in blood along the chassis. He put the
engine back on the track, turned on the power
to the DCC controller, and slowly started the locomotive. He sounded the whistle several times
as the locomotive went around the oval. He ran
it a little faster and even in the reverse direction.
It all looked and sounded fine to him.

"I'm sorry, Annie, I'm not sure what Eddie
was talking about. Let me have some time to
think about it. If it's okay with you, I'm going to

take the locomotive with me. In the meantime, please don't discuss what Eddie told you or tell anyone I took the locomotive."

Tom put the 2-8-0 into a generic train storage box and they left the basement. When they reached the front door, Annie softly grabbed his arm and turned him to face her. "I'm sorry, Tom. You're a good friend. I should have told you sooner how much I appreciate your support."

"Good night, Annie. You take care now."

I guess those are two names I can scratch off the list, Tom thought as the door closed behind him. It was only when Tom got into his truck that he realized that even if someone else had killed Eddie, it didn't mean that Annie couldn't have killed Bill. Maybe Eddie was blackmailing someone because Eddie had other dirt on him or her. With all the infidelities, possible embezzlement, thefts, and other sins that Tom had discovered beneath the placid surface of Pennsville, nothing else would surprise him at this point. If Eddie suspected Annie was a murderer, he would want to get as far away from her as possible and take Molly with him. Maybe Annie had him look at the locomotive as a test to see how much he knew. Dead men don't talk, but somehow he had to figure out how a dead man's locomotive could.

Sitting in his truck, Tom got that feathery feeling in his gut again that someone was staring at him. He surreptitiously glanced down the street and saw a car parked at the end of the block. As another car drove up the street, its headlights briefly reflected off the wire-frame glasses of an occupant in the driver's side. Tom was sure it was his mystery stalker. He started his truck and drove around the corner, parking on a parallel street. Tom grabbed a screwdriver out of his glove compartment and stuck it in his coat pocket. It wouldn't do him much good against a gun, but it was the best protection at hand.

Tom quietly crept up to the passenger side of the car and knocked on the window. If the driver was startled, he certainly didn't show it. Tom motioned with his finger, and the man rolled down the window.

"I don't know who you are or why you are following me, but it's about time we had a talk."

The man reached over toward a leather jacket on the passenger-side seat.

"Hold it right there," Tom shouted, pointing the screwdriver in his pocket at the man.

"Easy there," the man said. "I just want to get my business card. OK?"

"OK. Use two fingers and keep your other hand where I can see it."

The man passed a card out the window. Tom held it up to the streetlamp to read it, keeping one eye on the man. It simply said, "Charles Porter, Investigator, United Insurance." There was no address or website, just a phone number.

"Insurance? I don't understand."

"Do you think you can lower your pen or whatever it is you have in your pocket now?"

Tom sheepishly complied.

"I'd rather not have this conversation in the middle of the street. Do you know the Crossroads Diner?"

Tom nodded.

"Why don't you meet me there in 20 minutes and we can talk."

Tom was skeptical that Porter would show up, but his car was parked outside when Tom got there. Porter was sitting at a back booth with two glasses of water and menus spread out in front of him. One other booth was occupied by a gaggle of teenagers, satisfying their late-night munchies with milk shakes and cheeseburger platters. None of them even looked up at Tom as he passed by. They had mastered their generation's talent of eating with one hand while texting with the other, their eyes glued to their screens.

A tired-looking waitress limped over. Porter ordered a diet soda and French fries. Tom asked for a cup of decaf. He had had enough stimulation for one evening. Tom finally got a good look at his stalker under the bright fluorescent lights of the diner. Charles Porter had a medium build with thinning light brown hair and wire-rimmed glasses. Dressed in a faded flannel shirt, jeans, and a worn leather jacket, he looked like any suburban dad you would see rooting for his son at a Little League game or shopping at Home Depot.

"Yeah, I know. I'm not what you expected. We can't all be Sam Spade in a fedora and trench coat," Porter said, as if reading Tom's mind. "Besides, it helps in my line of work to blend in."

They fell silent as the waitress dropped off their orders, somehow sliding the drinks onto the table without spilling a drop. Porter poured a generous glop of ketchup onto his fries.

"So what exactly is your line of work, Mr.

Porter, and what does it have to do with me? I know you've been following me on and off since Bill Murphy's funeral."

"Please, call me Charlie. In a nutshell, I thought maybe you were the one who had knocked off one of United Insurance's clients, William J. Murphy."

Tom choked on a mouthful of ice water, turning red and gasping for breath. The concerned waitress started shuffling over, but Tom waved her away.

Charlie pretended not to notice and dug into his French fries.

When Tom got his breath back, Charlie continued. "Mr. Murphy had taken out a rather large life insurance policy about three months earlier, with a rider for some of his more expensive trains, including the Triplex. This was on top of the insurance he had through his union. Of course his being killed so soon after the insurance being bought was a red flag. A red flag means I get involved."

"I still don't see what this has to do with me. What would I have to gain by Bill's death?"

"You know in these types of situations we always look at the beneficiary, which of course in this case is his widow. We also look at someone who could be helping the widow. I know all about your wife Claire being in a nursing home. It's a real shame. It also would make it easy and even somewhat understandable for you to be having an affair with Bill's wife. Want one?" Charlie offered, pushing the half-eaten plate of fries toward Tom.

"No, thanks." Tom couldn't believe what he

was hearing. But it did make total sense, in a
sickening kind of way. "Please continue."

"You had plenty of opportunity to kill him
and then pretend you found the body, planning
ahead of time to make it look like a robbery. As
a model train guy, you would have grabbed the
Triplex because it was the most expensive item
there. I know that's what you told your friend,
Chief Taylor. You must have realized in retro-
spect that it looked suspicious, so you've been
trying to pin it on another modeler."

"And how would you know all this?"

"I'm an ex-cop. Let's just say I maintain excellent sources within state police departments."

"If I *am* the killer, why are you telling me all
this?"

"You and Mrs. Murphy conspiring together
was just my initial hypothesis. I always follow
the money, although sex and money often go
hand in hand. After some digging, I found out
about her relationship with Eddie Paxton. By
the way, I was watching Mrs. Murphy's house
tonight, not following you per se. It's possible
she could have been doing the unfortunate Mr.
Paxton while stringing you along, but that's not
what my instincts tell me."

"Well thank goodness for your instincts."

"Yeah, it's also what his autopsy report tells
me. United got a copy of that. It seems Mr.
Murphy had a heart aneurysm on top of his
high blood pressure. The timing of the insurance policy coincides with his last medical
exam. Even though he was scheduled for surgery
and his prognosis was good, he must have gotten spooked. Also, I spoke to his eldest daugh-

ter"—Charlie flipped through a small notebook he pulled from his jacket pocket—"Elizabeth. She's a nurse. Mr. Murphy had confided in her, but made her swear up and down not to tell her mother yet. Which means Mrs. Murphy never knew that she was going to be a widow probably sooner rather than later, so she had a motive. Still, I don't really see her bopping her husband over the head by herself. You, on the other hand, pose a challenge to finger as a conspirator."

"How so?" Tom was getting drawn into the investigator's narrative despite himself.

"Even with my best efforts to prove otherwise, you remain squeaky clean. From all accounts and my personal observations, you're totally devoted to your wife. It *almost* restores some of my faith in mankind. Plus, I was discreetly following you the day you lost your brakes and slid off the road. You looked uninjured, so I kept going. That incident points to the real killer trying to get you off his or her trail."

"Does this mean you know who tampered with my truck?" Tom asked eagerly.

"Unfortunately, they must have done it before I got there because I didn't see anyone near your truck. Now with Mr. Paxton killed, you off the table, and no other men—or women for that matter—romantically linked to her, I've hit a dead end with Mrs. Murphy."

"So you agree that Eddie's death was no accident," Tom jumped in.

"Maybe yes, maybe no. And between you, me, and the fencepost, I don't think Harvey Waite killed Mr. Murphy either. Mr. Waite is strictly small potatoes. I'm still here because my own personal curiosity about the killer demands to be satisfied. I'm not even billing these hours to United. A good investigator *should* be curious, but sometimes it can be a real pain in the ass."

"I'm finding that out for myself," Tom sympathized. "Let me ask you something else. Can you tell from the autopsy report whether the killer was right- or left-handed?"

"Inconclusive. Don't always believe those re-enactments they do on *CSI*. The person who swung that heavy toolbox most likely used both hands. Why do you ask?"

"It's part of the theory I'm working on. There are just too many missing pieces to put it all together yet."

Charlie unwrapped two sticks of Juicy Fruit gum and folded them into his mouth. "This is the only thing that keeps me from going back to smoking. My constant chewing drove my ex-wife crazy, another helpful thing about it," he said, winking at Tom. He abruptly switched gears. "What I don't get is why did Mrs. Murphy give you the small locomotive I saw you carry out of her house tonight? I know it isn't the Triplex."

"I think that locomotive might have been used by Eddie to blackmail the killer, but I have no idea how."

"Will you let me know what you find out? You can leave a message for me on the number on the card. The sooner I get this case totally wrapped up, the sooner I get out of this oh-so-fascinating town."

"Sure."

The waitress asked if they wanted anything

else and, without waiting for an answer, placed the bill on the table. Charlie brushed off Tom's offer of money and paid it, along with a generous tip.

"This one's on United. Just one more thing."

Uh-oh, thought Tom. Now that he has assured me of my innocence, here comes his alternative theory about my guilt to throw me off guard.

"I grew up on a small ranch in Oklahoma and remember sleek red-and-silver Santa Fe engines streaking through the fields in the distance. They were beautiful machines," Charlie said dreamingly. "I find myself a little envious of you model railroaders. My ex got the house, so I live in a one-bedroom apartment with a small office. Do you think there's any way I could set up some kind of model Santa Fe railroad?"

"I'm sure of it," Tom replied. "I knew a guy who built a whole layout that fit under his bed. Your job sounds stressful. Modeling would be just the thing to help you relax after a long day of chasing the bad guys."

"Sounds like a plan. I'll be in touch."

CHAPTER 28

Tom knew he was missing something that had happened on the day of the murder that Eddie had somehow picked up on. He sat down at his workbench and tried to remember the normal order of events that unfolded when Tom, James, Gordon, and Bill would prepare for the Christmas open house. This would be the third year that they had been doing it together.

He leaned over and absentmindedly rubbed the belly of a grateful Lady as he tried to concentrate. In his mind's eye he could see Bill opening the boxes that contained his locomotives and rolling stock while he kept a running banter with the rest of the crew. He usually had some snide remarks about James' supposed great wealth, calling him "Mr. One Percent." He would lament that a poor working stiff like himself couldn't afford any of James' collector items. Bill would tease Tom about his *Thomas & Friends* items, asking him when he would grow up and run real trains with the big boys. He reserved his most venomous "jokes" for Gordon, insulting his manhood in numerous subtle and not-so-subtle ways, often by bringing up Madge's leaving him. Gordon would remain his usual calm self and either mildly laugh or shrug his shoulders. Donnie would be watching any trains that were in motion, oblivious to everything else around him.

Suddenly an incident that had occurred at one of the club's open houses popped into his head. The modelers who had sound-equipped models would usually turn up the volume so that the whistles, horns, and chuffs could be heard above the crowds of boisterous children. They would wait to do that until Gordon had taken the sound-sensitive Donnie home. Once Bill had turned up the volume all the way on one of his locomotives just to upset Donnie and get a rise out of Gordon. Donnie had let out a series of ear-splitting screams and rushed around flapping his arms until Gordon had quickly but deliberately turned off the sound. Instead of upsetting Gordon, the shrill screaming had obviously hit a raw nerve with Bill, who had turned a bright red. He would always make sure he kept his sound down if Donnie was in the room.

Tom smacked his forehead. "Lady, your owner is an idiot." Lady wagged her tail as if in agreement.

He ran the Consolidation on his own test track. Just as he suspected, the sound had been turned way down. He hadn't paid attention to the sound level at Annie's house. Even if Eddie wasn't there to witness the incident at the open house, Tom was sure he knew that Bill would have the sound way down if Donnie was in the vicinity. Bill had been kidded about it for years. Eddie had evidently heard from Annie enough about what had happened at the church that day to put two and two together. If the locomotive "proved" Gordon and Donnie had been there with Bill, then Gordon had been acting when he showed up around the same time as James and pretended to be surprised about Bill's murder. However, there was still no direct evidence linking them to the murder. It was possible that Gordon, the ever-protective father, just did not want the police to know that Donnie had been there earlier. They could have left the church for some reason before Bill was murdered. Unfortunately, a smoking steam locomotive was not the proverbial smoking gun, even if it had cost Eddie his life. Tom still needed proof before Ben had enough evidence to arrest the murderer.

It was clear to Tom that the root motivation for two such senseless deaths was the killer's obsession, whatever that may be. People often thought that modeling was an obsession, but Tom had learned that everyone had an obsession of some kind—from Earl's urge to possess historical documents to Gordon's fanatical need to protect his son to his own dogged pursuit of Bill's murder, even when it had proved life-threatening. Tom had to figure out a way to back Gordon into a corner, which would force him to confess what had led to Bill's murder. He knew he would need some backup but couldn't risk having any police there to spook the killer. If he couldn't call in the cavalry, he decided he had the next best thing—ex-Marine and high-tech expert Percy. He would just have to convince Percy that his plan would work.

CHAPTER 29

The lead story on the local news that night was the arrest of Earl Stanley Winston III for suspected trafficking in stolen historical documents. Earl tried to duck from cameramen as he was being led in to his arraignment, his jacket tossed over his arms in a vain attempt to hide the handcuffs. Tom did a double-take. Earl had dyed his hair a mousy brown and shaved off his mustache. There was no mistaking his Southern-tinged, pedantic voice as he protested his innocence.

"Gentlemen, I can assure you all that this is just a big misunderstanding. It's no crime to love history," he shouted into the mikes thrust in his direction as a police officer firmly led him up the courtroom steps.

"Earl Stanley Winston III, a professor emeritus from Lehigh University, was arrested at 3:00 this afternoon at Philadelphia International Airport, attempting to board a plane to Mexico City," the news anchor stated. "He was wanted in connection with the theft of historical documents."

The phone rang. "I assume you saw that the old goat got arrested," a voice gushed without any preliminaries. Tom recognized the voice of Caroline Trevors, sounding much more sober than the last time they spoke.

"I was just watching the news now."

"My sister is a reporter for the *Philadelphia Inquirer*, so she let me in on some details. The FBI White Collar Crimes Unit had been watching some fence who trafficked in historical documents on the Dark Web for a while."

"I'm sorry, the what web?"

"The Dark Web," Caroline answered. "It's the section of the Internet utilized by criminals that lets them keep their anonymity. Anyway, our favorite history professor tried to sell the Mary Todd Lincoln letter to the fence. Since the feds knew the provenance of the letter, they were able to connect it to him and track him to the sale rendezvous. Voila, they got their fence, but somehow the professor got away. He didn't get far, though, lame disguise or no lame disguise. It seems a search warrant of the professor's house turned up a treasure trove of stolen documents. He wasn't stealing to sell the items for profit but rather for his own personal collection. However, he needed to get his hands on a pile of cash fast to try some supposed stem cell cure for Parkinson's offered by a quack clinic down in Mexico. Since the letter was written by Mary Todd Lincoln, whom the professor never really liked, he decided he could part with it. Big mistake. Although maybe getting caught was ironically the best thing for him since the Mexican clinic would have taken him for everything he had and left him in worse health. Now that pompous ass will have to take his chances with the federal prison medical system. The even better news is that the board realized the theft wasn't *my* fault, so all has been forgiven. I'm on my way out to meet the other historical archivists burned by Professor Winston for some celebratory Mexican food and margaritas. Viva la feds! Thanks again for your help. Ciao." Ms. Trevors hung up before Tom could get a word in edgewise.

Tom finally called Gordon at 10:00 pm. Although Tom had written a script for what he wanted to say so he could sound convincing, he was so nervous that the words rushed out of him in a torrent.

"I think you know why I'm calling. I know Donnie killed Bill. I'm sure it was an accident, but you've made things much worse by covering up for him."

"If you are so sure, why haven't you told your friend Ben?"

"I also know Eddie was blackmailing you. I have the Consolidation. You and Donnie had to have been in the church basement *before* the murder because Bill lowered the sound. We usually increase the sound for the Christmas display, but that loud volume would have bothered Donnie."

"That's what *you* claim," Gordon said calmly. "But I always pegged you as a real straight arrow. I would think you would have run to the Chief right away with any evidence. You haven't told him your theory yet, have you?"

"No, I haven't told him. The ugly truth is, I need money to pay for Claire's nursing care. It's incredibly expensive. I don't know how much longer I can afford it, and I'm afraid of what will happen when I run out of money," Tom said in a choked voice. He did not need to fake sounding anguished because it was not that far from reality.

"You know how I deal with blackmailers. Aren't you taking a big chance coming after me?"

"Eddie was greedy and stupid. I'm going to take the $10,000 you are going to give me so Claire and I can move to Phoenix to be near my son and his family. I'll give you the Consolidation, so I won't have any way to ask for more money. You can take it apart or destroy it and no one will be the wiser. But for some insurance, I have a letter in my safe deposit box that will implicate you if anything happens to me before I leave town."

"Okay. But I need some time to get that much money together. I don't have large sums of cash just lying around."

"You have until tomorrow night, New Year's Eve. I'm sure you're not going anywhere to celebrate."

"Meet me at the shop at 11:30 pm and make sure you bring the Consolidation. If I see the Chief or any other cops, the deal is off. And it won't be you I'm after, it will be your precious Claire."

CHAPTER 30

Tom turned the knob of the back door to the store. The door was unlocked. As he stepped in, it took a few seconds for his eyes to adjust to the dimness of the store, which was lit by only a single fluorescent ceiling fixture in the front. The front blinds were drawn, so even the faint light afforded by the streetlights was filtered out. When Gordon suddenly emerged from the shadows, Tom jumped. His heart started racing when he realized the black cylinder in Gordon's hand was not a steam locomotive but a gun.

"Lock the door and then move over here in front of me," Gordon ordered, pointing the gun at him. Gordon's voice was hard and commanding. When Tom looked at Gordon's face under the light, he could see that any trace of the gentle, self-effacing Gordon that he knew was gone and had been replaced by a stranger who looked quite capable of killing him.

"OK. Start walking to that doorway and go downstairs, slowly."

When they got downstairs, Tom heard the faint chuff-chuff of a sound-equipped K4 4-6-2 Pacific steam locomotive making its rounds on the clinic layout. Gordon must have been testing it while he was waiting for Tom.

"Where's Donnie?" Tom managed to croak. His mouth felt cotton dry.

"He's home safe and sound. And he's not going anywhere, with you or anyone else."

"Don't worry. It's not Donnie I want."

"What do you mean? Aren't you here to tell me how you know Donnie killed Bill?"

"But it wasn't Donnie, it was you," Tom replied angrily. He couldn't keep the outrage out of his voice. It really galled him that Gordon was willing to put the blame on his defenseless son. It gave him the courage to continue talking.

"In the shock and confusion of finding Bill's body, I never thought about the fact that you arrived late at the church. You and Donnie always arrived like clockwork. But it was the left-handed layout of the tools that gave you away, even before I got my hands on the Consolidation that Eddie was blackmailing you with. It meant that it was Donnie, not you, who was using the tools in your workshop. I was always so impressed that you had the time and energy to run the store, take care of Donnie, and still turn out these gorgeous dioramas and amazing weathered locos and cars. I don't believe you forced Donnie to slave away at your modeling projects. I'll bet you probably couldn't *stop* Donnie once he got going. With his meticulous, obsessive methods of production and your expertise and imagination, you had a can't-lose formula for winning modeling contests, getting your MMR, and boosting your business. But it wasn't just about the business, was it? Winning all those contests put you in center stage. You were finally *somebody*, with a dedicated fan base looking up to you." Tom slowly moved around the track as he was talking. "Bill must have somehow threatened to take it all away."

"He thought he was so funny," Gordon exploded. "Who's laughing now?" Gordon let out a chilling cackle.

"Bill always teased me about Madge leaving, implying I wasn't a 'real man.' He called Donnie a retard." Gordon snorted. "Donnie probably has twice the IQ of that dimwit Bill. When I met him at the church that morning, the first words out of his mouth were, 'If it isn't the mouse and the retard who supplies all the mouse's cheese.' Somehow he had also figured out that Donnie had been doing the majority of my modeling work. You know, at first having Donnie do small projects was a way of keeping him busy while I closed up the shop at night. Most people don't realize how much work is involved in keeping a store like this running. But Donnie was so good at detail work and liked it so much, as long as he could do things precisely and in *his* order, that he was soon doing a large chunk of all my modeling work. It made me feel proud of my son." Gordon's face softened for a minute. "You know that no matter what I've done, I've always tried to be a good father."

"I do know that you love your son. But I still don't understand *why* you killed Bill," Tom admitted, desperate to keep Gordon talking.

"I was tired of his insults. He thought he was such a big deal. You should have seen his face when I told him all about Annie and Eddie carrying on behind his back. One advantage to blending into the wallpaper is that I see and hear things because no one notices I'm around. I caught Annie and Eddie making out behind the Quik Chek one time. They looked up and saw the intruder was me and went right back at it. After all, who ever felt threatened by good old Gordon? I told Bill, 'I guess your buddies at the Acme and the American Legion would be interested in hearing all the sordid details.'"

"'You wouldn't dare do that,' Bill had yelled. His face was redder than his snowman's crimson scarf. 'How do you think the NMRA would react if they found out who *really* did your modeling work? You'd lose your MMR, all your trophies, and a big chunk of your business. It would just be you and the retard.'"

"Something in me snapped. I don't even remember hitting him with the toolbox. I told Donnie that Bill was a bad man who wanted to hurt me and if Donnie told anyone, I would go away forever, just like his mother. Of course Donnie doesn't know that I had taken care of his mother. We had it out that night when she thought she would be running off with Harvey, only she found out that Harvey had taken off without her. This was after she had drained all her private accounts and given the money to Harvey for 'traveling expenses,' including a nest egg of stock she had inherited from her parents. She was furious and said some things about me that I won't repeat. When she saw my face, she became frightened and tried to make it up by throwing her arms around me. I strangled her with my bare hands and buried her about right below where we're standing. Madge had always told me that I could expand the trains section over her dead body. Well, she was right." Gordon laughed eerily again. "Once we tore everything up past here with my major renovations, no one ever noticed that a section of the concrete in the original storeroom had been redone."

Tom had maneuvered himself to a spot where he could feel the DCC controller on the layout behind him. "Planting the Triplex on Harvey, that was a neat trick, maybe a little too neat. I figured you wanted to kill two birds with one stone: get your revenge against the man who stole your wife while making him take the fall for Bill's murder."

"Everyone just assumed that Madge had run off with Harvey. All I had to do was play the aggrieved husband. It actually increased business in the store. Maybe having a murder in the store would help business again," Gordon said with a sickening smile. "Too bad they can't find your body here. I'm sorry, Tom. I've always liked you. But you just know too much now to let you go. You should have quit after I cut your brakes. By the way, I know your supposed protection letter is a bluff. I used my safety deposit box yesterday and casually asked Erin at the bank if she had seen you lately. She said it had been a while. I've typed up a nice note for Chief Taylor explaining how you can't deal with Claire's deteriorating condition and need some time away. You were just too upset to talk to him about it. I traced your signature from your credit card receipt. I did a great job, if I may say so myself. Now it's time you and your annoying investigation were derailed."

As Gordon raised his arm to shoot, Tom jabbed at the controller, hoping he could hit the right buttons. The K4 let out the piercing whistle that had earned it the nickname "the screaming banshee." It startled Gordon and he shot off balance, hitting Tom in the right shoulder. Tom leapt forward and managed to bring Gordon down to the ground with him. As they rolled on the ground, Tom struggled to get the gun out of Gordon's hand, even as he felt a blinding pain in his shoulder.

"Police. Hold it right there," Ben shouted, as he rushed in with his weapon drawn. Two more armed officers were right behind him.

Gordon stood up. He took one look at the Chief's face and dropped his gun.

"Cuff him, read him his rights, and get him out of here," Ben said to his officers. "And be careful, behind that meek store clerk face lies a stone-cold killer."

Ben gently helped Tom off the ground and onto a nearby chair. "Tom, I think that has to be about the worst tackle I ever saw."

"Ben, not that I'm not happy to see you, but Percy was supposed to be covering my back. Wasn't he recording the whole conversation?"

Percy came running into the basement at full speed, almost crashing into the layout. "What happened? I thought I heard gunshots." He looked at his ashen-faced friend. "I don't know whether to hug you or hit you over your damn stubborn head with that locomotive. I can't believe you talked me into going along with this."

"Glad to see you too, Percy. And please don't harm that little locomotive. Its whistle helped save my life."

"Well, luckily your friend Percy here has more common sense than you. He let me know about your harebrained scheme to get Gordon to confess with him recording every word broadcast through your cell phone. I was sitting in his car with him and heard enough of your conversation to know you were in trouble. Sorry to cut it so close. I already radioed for an ambulance."

They could hear a wailing siren getting closer. In the background were the muffled blasts of New Year's Eve celebrants setting off firecrackers.

Ben reached into the small first-aid kit he carried on his belt. "Here, press this pad against your wound."

Tom looked down and was surprised to see his shoulder bleeding profusely. "It's a good thing Claire is not here to see this. She'd kill me," he told his friends with a smile.

"She'd have to get in line," Percy angrily muttered.

The ambulance arrived and two emergency technicians rushed over to treat Tom before Percy had a chance to scold him again.

Tom opened his eyes later New Year's Day to see Charlie Porter sitting in his hospital room's visitor's chair, perusing a copy of *Model Railroad Planning* while furiously chewing gum. Tom was still groggy and his shoulder was throbbing after the operation needed to remove the bullet. While he slept after the operation, he had felt a woman's hand on his wrist. "Claire, you've come to take care of me," he moaned. He tried to reach out to her before he realized it was a nurse, checking his pulse.

Tom wasn't surprised that Charlie had somehow found a way to infiltrate a patient's room that was supposed to be off limits to everyone but immediate family. "Do you think you could pass me over that cup of water," Tom croaked.

"You were supposed to contact me if you figured out who the killer was," Charlie complained.

"I wasn't 100% positive until last night. A good engineer likes to test and then test again. I would have called you today if I hadn't been a little bit indisposed," Tom said as he gingerly sat up and accepted the cup from Charlie.

"Good morning, Mr. McCloud," a nurse chirped as she entered the room. Tom realized it was Elizabeth, Annie's daughter. She was carrying a vase bursting with yellow chrysanthemums.

"This is just a small token of appreciation from our entire family. We're so grateful for your help in catching Dad's killer. My mother was beside herself when she heard you got shot."

"Do I need an invitation or can anyone join this party?" Chief Taylor asked as he strode into the room. Charlie gave him a friendly wave.

Elizabeth took note of Charlie lounging in the chair. "I'm not sure who you are or what you are doing here, but I won't call security this time. You both have five minutes more. Mr. McCloud needs his rest," she said firmly. She gave Charlie one more baleful look and left the room.

"I just dropped in to see how the patient was doing," Ben said. "You look better than anyone should who has just been shot. Oh yeah, I have a message from Percy. Rest assured, he's taking care of Lady until you get home. He hopes it's soon because Lady is quite distressed at your absence. I think that's his way of saying he's upset about your shooting too. Well, I've got to get going. I still have lots of paperwork to fill out about Gordon's three murders."

"I guess I better get out of here before Nurse Ratched returns," Charlie said. "You know, for a civilian, you did a good job of solving this case, except, of course, for getting shot. I could use a brain like yours for bouncing ideas off of. Why don't you come work with me when you're feeling better? It would involve some traveling, but you could name your own hours."

"Thanks, but no thanks. I've had my fill of investigating."

"Would you at least help me with setting up my layout? Your under-the-bed setup is a good idea, but now I'm thinking about building one along the walls of my office."

"That's something I would be happy to help you with."

Once everyone left, Tom drifted off to sleep. Tom dreamt that he and Claire were enjoying a delicious picnic lunch along the banks of a tranquil river. A Triplex locomotive was chugging along on track paralleling the river, a plume of soft gray smoke silhouetted against the bright blue sky. As the cab went past, the smiling engineer tipped his cap and tooted a friendly whistle blast. The demon train had been vanquished forever.

Epilogue

Tom drove down Main Street admiring with fresh eyes the oaks wreathed in green leaves that lined the street. He had returned to Pennsville a couple of days ago after visiting his new grandson, Thomas Clareton McCloud, in Arizona. Tom enjoyed the visit, but he was glad to be back home for many reasons. He had humored Doug and Stephanie by checking out a few retirement communities near them, but he wasn't ready to move to the desert yet. There was something to be said for living someplace with four seasons. He was looking forward to meeting Ben for coffee and assuring his old friend that he wasn't going anywhere yet.

On the way to the Busy Bee, he had taken a slight detour to drive past Annie's house. It had a "Sold" sign from Pennsville Realty on the front lawn and a moving van in the driveway. Annie had insisted on driving him home when he was discharged from the hospital after the shooting. She regularly visited him throughout January, filling his refrigerator with quarts of chicken soup and doing housework chores despite his protests. She told him it was her way of thanking him for bringing Bill's killer to justice.

Tom didn't need the help or want Annie to feel obligated to him, but he realized all the fussing over him made Annie feel less guilty about him getting shot. By February, Annie had decided to move to Tampa, FL, to be closer to her mother, who was in failing health. She told Tom she felt haunted in Pennsville by bad memories. Even working at the Quik Chek, with its association with Eddie, had become too painful. She needed a fresh start somewhere else. Tom told her to do whatever made sense for her and wished her the best of luck. Before he left for Arizona, Annie made Tom promise he would visit her in Tampa someday.

Hank had visited while Tom was home recuperating. At the next model train club meeting, Tom was happy to notify the members that H. Murphy and Sons Construction were volunteering time and materials to build the benchwork for housing the new model railroad layout at the Children's Hospital. The club used Earl's previously supplied plan as a blueprint for the layout. The Murphy crew had placed it at the perfect eye level for children in wheelchairs. There was a plaque on the case commemorating the Bill Murphy Memorial Railroad. Annie made a generous donation to stock it and pay for maintenance. Annie also donated Bill's circus train to the local Boy Scouts troop. Several troop members were working on their Railroad Merit badge and were delighted to have such a fun project to complete. Tom was going to contact the scoutmaster. Tom hoped that once the train was done, the scouts would help him set it up at the Good Shepherd for the enjoyment of the residents. He knew Bill would be pleased if his train found a good home.

Besides trains on the move, the wheels of justice were spinning as winter had morphed into spring. Gordon took a plea bargain and agreed to three consecutive life sentences to avoid the death penalty. Professor Winston also entered a plea deal. He was still on the hook for some prison time, but in exchange for a reduced sentence, he agreed to lend his expertise to the FBI to authenticate stolen historical documents. Tom knew if Ms. Trevors could have had anything to say about it, the professor would have been displayed in stocks on Independence Mall as a deterrent for would-be document thieves.

Tom had called Isabelle before he left for Arizona to tell her about the birth of his and Claire's new grandson. She had been only too willing to share the latest news about the Spencers after assuring Tom that she did not gossip, not like *some* residents of Pennsville.

"Did you know that James got probation for embezzling the Volunteer Firefighters' funds after he promised to pay everything back? The insurance company declined to pursue him for insurance fraud since he returned the claim money for Emily's supposedly stolen jewelry, with interest. The Spencers had to sell some assets and are living more frugally, but it seems to have made James bearable to be around. Don't you agree?" She continued without giving Tom a chance to answer. "I heard Emily is faithfully attending Gamblers Anonymous meetings. She even put herself on the ban list at the casino. That shopping diva is spending most of her time these days as a volunteer teaching tennis to underprivileged youth."

"Well I'm glad some good came out of all their problems," Tom replied.

"Oh, did you read that Harvey Waite was extradited to face larceny charges in New York? Once his arrest hit social media, I understand women came out of the woodwork from up and down the East Coast to accuse him of fleecing them out of money. I'm not sure what all those women saw in that lounge lizard," Isabelle sniffed.

"Not everyone can be as perceptive as you, dear Isabelle."

Tom wasn't sure if it was his uncharacteristic flattery that had rendered Isabelle speechless or if she had run out of juicy news to share. Tom took advantage of the lull to send his regards to Butch and get off the phone. He would have to find a way to prevent Isabelle from corralling him for an interrogation about the shooting when he saw her at the annual Memorial Day family barbeque. It probably would be easier to dam Niagara Falls than stop her flow of questions.

As Tom pulled into a parking spot near the Busy Bee, he noticed Ryan leaving the hobby shop across the street with a couple of bulging bags. It looked like Ryan had turned into a full-blown model train addict. Charlie also had plunged whole-heartedly into the hobby. Charlie was too impatient to wait for Tom's help. He had done his homework and created a new layout in his apartment on his own. Tom had been impressed by the photographs Charlie had emailed him.

Tom joined Ben at the Chief's usual booth. Once he got a welcome-back hug from Molly and their coffee mugs had been filled, the beaming grandfather pulled out pictures of the newborn to show off to an appreciative Ben.

"He weighed a hefty 8 pounds, 10 ounces," Tom bragged. "I bet he'll be an even better football player than his Poppy."

"Speaking of tacklers, I see that wing of yours must be healed since you're no longer favoring it. Is it still giving you any pain?"

"It's fine. I stopped by Pennsville Toy and Hobby Store yesterday," Tom noted, anxious to change the topic. Everyone, including Ben, seemed to think he was a big-time hero for getting shot, which was ridiculous. "I was glad to see that Madge's widowed sister, Marion, has moved to Pennsville and is running the business." He didn't tell Ben that it had taken some time for him to find the courage to visit the hobby shop since he still felt a little spooked by his encounter with Gordon.

"After we dug up and processed Madge's body to use as evidence against Gordon, Marion at least had the solace of giving her sister a proper burial. She had always felt something was wrong when Madge never got in touch with her while supposedly on the run with Harvey."

"Marion told me she moved into her sister's house and is taking care of Donnie. It's hard on him with Gordon in prison, but at least the rest of his routine is intact. In a change of *my* routine, I'm taking Percy on a fishing trip next month as a small repayment for all the help he gave me. And just so he doesn't get it in his head that this means he's finally convinced me that fishing is the ultimate hobby, I gave one of his nephews some track and his first locomotive. I hope he drives his Uncle Percy crazy asking for more trains."

Ben chuckled. "I hear business is actually booming since Marion hired an assistant, Owen, to set up and run an online site for the store. True to this town's form, tongues are already wagging that Owen seems to be working an awful lot of late nights," Ben added.

"I'm glad to see that the citizens of Pennsville haven't changed that much." Tom held up his mug in a mock salute to the regulars at the counter.

Ben raised his hand for a refill, but Molly was busy flirting with Owen as he waited at the register for a take-out coffee.

"It looks like our favorite waitress has moved on also."

"Speaking of moving on, I have to get going," Tom said rising.

"Where are you rushing off to? Do you have another murder to solve?" Ben teased.

"No more murders for me. I'm off to visit the prettiest girl in town."

About the Authors

DEBRA SCHIFF works for Bachmann Trains and lives in Philadelphia. This is her first novel.

MIKE BLUMENSAADT is a retired photographer and N scale modeler who lives in San Francisco.